T0285710

CINDERWICH

CHERIE PRIEST

APEX BOOK COMPANY | LEXINGTON, KY

This is a work of fiction. All of the characters, organizations, and events portrayed in this novella are either products of the author's imagination or are used fictitiously.

CINDERWICH

Copyright © 2024 by Cherie Priest

ISBN (softcover) 978-1-955765-20-6
ISBN (epub) 978-1-955765-21-3
ISBN (Kindle) 978-1-955765-25-1

Cover art by Daniele Sera
Cover design by Mikio Murikami
Edited by Jason Sizemore

Visit us online at ApexBookCompany.com.

First Edition: 2024

For Quinn

CHAPTER ONE

THE FIRST ELLEN THRUSH has probably been dead all this time—and it's not that I don't care, exactly. I care, I think. I'm curious at least. But thank God, no one expects me to get too worked up about it. She vanished before I was born, and all I have of her is an old picture or two and her name. My mother gave it to me when I was born: two years, one month, and thirteen days after Ellen mailed a Christmas card to my grandmother. In it, she wrote that she was happy and wished the family a wonderful new year.

There's evidence to suggest she didn't mean the last part, but it's not for me to say. Maybe she was a bigger person than I am.

Frankly, I'd be surprised.

We are too much alike, as my mother and grandmother have never failed to remind me. When I did good things—when I finished my master's degree, when I bought my house with my own money—then I was so very much like my long-lost Aunt Ellen. She had such an independent spirit after all! But when I did things the Thrushes didn't like, somehow it was still the same story: when I dropped out of my doctorate program, when I got a DUI, when I came home with a girl instead of a boy. Oh yes. So much like my no-good, pervert of an aunt, may she rest in peace wherever she lies.

That's when they'd pretend that I never switched to using my middle name. They'd call me by her name, with a sneer just loud enough to be heard. Even after I got my sober-for-a-year chip. (I shouldn't have bothered. I threw it away.) Even after I brought home another boy or two, like I was trying to maintain a balance on some ledger, it never seemed to matter.

So I don't see the Thrushes very much—not anymore. I didn't go missing like Aunt Ellen; I just quit coming home.

Plenty of people said that's exactly what Ellen did; she ran away from home, if you can call it that when a woman's an adult in her twenties. But I don't believe it. Sure, I fantasized more than once about walking away from Thrush House myself, leaving behind everyone who ever called it home. Of course, I understand the urge to quit arguing, to quit participating in the endless escalation of whose feelings are hurt most, and why, and by whom. Absolutely, they are exhausting women who deserve one another.

I can truly imagine there's a world where my aunt Ellen might have had it up to here, packed a suitcase, and rode off into the sunset with her thesis advisor slash girlfriend—an esteemed professor of women's history at Vanderbilt University in Nashville.

But not this world. I don't believe that Ellen ran away, and I don't believe that she's alive anymore either.

I don't believe she would have abandoned Judith.

———

The first time I met Judith, she said I could call her "Aunt Judy" if I wanted, but I wasn't having it. This random woman was no old friend or near relation; she'd looked me up out of the blue after spotting my name on a form. By sheer coincidence, I was applying for a graduate program in history at the University of Florida, where she was working by then. I was hoping to pull together a thesis that made half an ounce of sense, and I wasn't entirely sure it was worth the trouble.

I'd been waitlisted and then called up.

I'd been spotted by Dr. Judith Kane, notably less esteemed in some regards since she'd run off with one of her students in the 1970s—or that was the campus rumor, as I was to later learn. I could've confirmed it for every gossiping undergrad, but I restrained myself. No one needed to know that she ran away with my aunt Ellen.

By all reports, Ellen was a legend. She was also a hellion and a heathen, but Judith would be the first one to tell you that, smiling over a cigarette, beside a glass of wine, in front of the fireplace when we were supposed to be talking about Aphra Behn and Elizabeth Carey.

It was never weird, sitting in her living room, surrounded by books, notes, booze, and the vague confidence that I wasn't going to finish my academic program any more than the first Ellen Thrush had ever finished hers. Our relationship was never inappropriate, either; though over time, I do admit I developed an attachment to Judith that might be described (by some nosy people, somewhere) as "unhealthy." I looked up to her, in a way I'd never looked up to any other woman before—no relative, mentor, or anyone else. Judith is brilliant, you see. She is beautiful. She is plenty old enough to be my mother, and for a few years, she was the most important person in my life.

You could say I had a crush, though that wouldn't quite be true. I didn't want to fuck her; I wanted to be her.

Don't worry. She didn't want to fuck me, either. She just wanted to believe that some little piece of her beloved Ellen lived on, or that someone else remembered her—even someone who'd never met her.

"I do think she died before you were born," she told me once.

"Because she would have never left you?"

She opened her mouth, and I thought she was going to say, "Yes, that's why." But she didn't. She took another draw of smoke and said, "No real reason at all, but it's very romantic, isn't it? The thought that she died and you were born; even your tragic family thought it meant something to give you her name. What if some other piece of her traveled with you? Some … awareness or spark of personality could've come along for the ride, following the name or following the next child to be born in a familiar family."

She lost me there. "You know enough about the Thrushes to call them tragic, but not enough to know … well. If the consciousness of Ellen Thrush survived at all, on any plane, the last place she'd ever go is home. Trust me on that one."

I remember how Judith had soured. "What if she was trying to … to …" Another sip. Tobacco and wine. "Find her way back to me.

What then?" She stared down at the smoldering stub that should've been put out already. She swapped it for the wine and gazed into the glass like she was an oracle; the cheap grocery store red came from the omphalos of Delphi itself.

God, I'd felt like an asshole. I think I muttered something along the lines of, "There must have been an easier way," but it wasn't the right thing to say. There was no right thing to say.

Judith Kane did not really believe in reincarnation, anyway. Not like she believed in old poetry.

Anyway, I did leave the program, as anyone who knew me might have guessed. Eventually, I left Florida too. And Judith. It was a tearful parting, one that seemed so full of dramatic inevitability at the time, but was probably just a tantrum in retrospect. Judith had wanted something I couldn't give her, and someone I couldn't be; she knew, before I even said so, that I was tired of reading about other people's great works and felt the need to create my own.

It was an ambitious tantrum, but it never went anywhere. I never wrote the Great American Novel or even reviewed one. I didn't get into hard-hitting journalism, or take any major stands against injustice, or do anything much to improve the world at large. I ended up an overloaded adjunct, teaching composition at the University of Tennessee. They'll put it on my tombstone: "She taught freshmen the five-paragraph essay." And that's all, I guess.

At first, Judith and I stayed in touch. We had to, after all the vehement vows and clutched hands and carefully worded promises.

But time and distance did their thing.

In those early professional years, I was in over my head, juggling a teaching schedule that should've been illegal for its casual cruelty. I was abrupt. I had my head up my own ass, as she told me more than once.

She was somehow both distant and needy in phone calls, then letters, and then the occasional email. Each Christmas card felt more perfunctory, and in the end, I stopped sending cards to anyone—just to avoid sending one to her and making it seem personal.

I don't know why it went strange that way. I don't know if I regret it, or if it was only the best and most productive use of everyone's time: for me to remove myself from a situation that felt, at times, like a spiraling dive into someone else's life. Judith was the archivist of all things Ellen, dedicating closets and crates to the study of what used to be and what might have been. For every new hint or scrap, she would make room if she didn't have room. (I think she'd always been making room for me—for exactly this reason.)

I couldn't escape the first Ellen's shadow, no matter how far I ran from our family. No matter how far I ran from our teacher.

Maybe it just wasn't in the cards.

Or maybe I was wrong, and the timing was wrong too; it'd been twelve years since I abandoned the graduate program and five years since I'd last heard from Judith when she sent me a new email. The subject line was cautiously cool: "I know it's been a while, but I wanted to show you this." Acknowledging that we hadn't spoken. Hinting at something shared.

Damn, she was good.

"Must be something to do with Ellen," I assumed out loud.

I didn't open the email right away but left my desk to go make a cup of coffee. I wanted to have my hands full when I clicked to see what olive branch she was offering, if that's what this was. She hadn't wronged me and she didn't owe me anything. If anyone owed anybody an olive branch, it was me—but I wasn't sure. If I was, I wouldn't have needed the coffee to steel myself against some apology or some request for an apology that was implied but never asked.

I shouldn't have worried. Judith was all business—if that's what the first Ellen had become to us.

I realize that this message comes out of the blue, but I wasn't sure who else I ought to approach. I hope you won't be upset or offended, and I pray that I'm not overstepping some unspoken boundary. I know that my Ellen was both what drew us together, and likely what pushed us apart. But she's what we had in common, then and now, and always.

I'm sure it won't surprise you to know that I've always kept one eye on the internet with regards to Ellen and whatever became of her. Science marches apace and cold cases are revived every day. Why not hers? Why not some fresh bit of evidence, lost for the decades and spotted again free of context, until and unless I successfully connect the dots?

It's always been a longshot, and I'm well aware that nothing is ever likely to come of such digital fishing, but something truly intriguing has come to my attention, and I wanted to bring it to yours.

In short, I've attached a link to a newspaper article—a little "local color" piece that recently appeared in the Chattanooga Times-Free Press. I cannot say and do not know if it's a reference to our Ellen, but it's certainly an intriguing set of coincidences, isn't it? The dates work out nicely—or horribly, however you prefer to think of it —and it's not so far away from where we last saw her.

Please, indulge me. Read the article and get back to me, if you would be so kind. I want a second opinion from someone who knows as much about the situation as I do. Am I reading too far into this? Am I finding hope where there's nothing but a tragic old mystery? Dear God, they even lost this poor woman's corpse ... it's not like there's any closure waiting at the other end, even if it turns out that this is our Ellen.

I'd like to go find this town, Kate—this tiny, ridiculous town. It's barely on Google Maps, just a wide spot in the road, as they say. But there's a little hotel and what's left of Main Street. Clearly, there are a few old timers still hanging around, willing to speak with the press. And someone, somewhere, who keeps leaving that spooky graffiti all over the damn place. In the same handwriting, even, after all these decades. The persistent vandal must be my age, at least. That's a clue, isn't it?

So yes, I'd like to visit Cinderwich, but I don't wish to do so alone. Could I possibly persuade you to join me there? I'll go with or without you, but I'd much rather have the company.

On a practical note, it would be helpful to have one of Ellen's family members on hand; it might mean fewer awkward questions, in a rural southern place that might or might not be caught up to the 21st century when it comes to LGBTQIA+ normalcy and whatnot. (Unless I'm being ungenerous, which is always possible.) If you're the one leading the inquiries, no one will find it strange. That's all I mean.

On a more personal note, I've missed you. I'd like to see you again. This will be an emotional and difficult trip for me, and I know you will understand better than anyone, despite the years and miles between us.

I'll be flying into Chattanooga this Friday, and I have a room booked in Cinderwich at the Rockford Inn. At the risk of being presumptuous, I requested a room with two double beds, in case you will do me the kindness of joining me there. If you won't, then I guess I've got plenty of room to unpack and spread out. But I'd rather have your presence.

She signed off with a simple, "Yours, Judith."

The article link was attached beneath her signature. The headline read, "Decades Old Mystery Refuses to Die". Ah, yes. Just a month until Halloween, so 'twas the season for such fluff pieces—in publications large and small, respected and frivolous.

I surrendered to the clickbait and loaded up the page.

"Who put Ellen in the blackgum tree?" That's the question still being asked via spray-paint, in the tiny town of Cinderwich, Tennessee. It's been 45 years since an unidentified woman's body was found wedged into the fork of a tree where she'd been at rest for at least two or three years (according to estimates at the time). Trespassing children spied her dress and a single shoe. Police retrieved the corpse and sent it out for an autopsy. No cause of death was ever determined, and no one ever came forward to claim the woman's remains. She had curly dark blonde hair and was approximately twenty years old. To date, her identity remains entirely unknown.

Or does it? One week after the mystery woman was removed from her resting place, a singular message appeared on the side of a barn nearby: "Who put Ellen in the blackgum tree?"

No one has any good answer, least of all if the woman's name was, in fact, Ellen. But the same query, written again and again in the very same handwriting, has appeared every year since 1979.most recently scrawled across the back of the town's historic train station ...

The rest of the article was heavy on atmosphere, light on details.

As Judith had mentioned, the corpse had been lost to the sands of time and so had the autopsy report from the hospital in Chattanooga, but there had been a few theories regarding her identity. Someone said that she was a prostitute from Franklin who'd gone missing around that same time, but that woman had later turned up alive. Someone else was confident that she was the victim of a serial killer who'd never been caught. A third "expert" suggested that she might have been the daughter of a prominent politician who'd gone in search of an abortion and never made it back. (But that was a Sue Ellen, not an Ellen. Important distinction, in my opinion.)

But at the end of the day, nobody had a clue who she was, how she died, or how she got in the blackgum tree.

No one except for the mystery vandal, if the graffiti wasn't the work of some corny prankster.

The academic corner of my mind, the bit of me that still demanded citations for casual assertions, had some concerns about the story. There wasn't much to suggest that it was true, in any version. Only the original news bulletins, some alleged scraps of paperwork from the coroner, and one page of a surviving police report suggested that the woman in the tree had ever existed at all.

Nothing but graffiti suggested that her name had been Ellen.

And the timing was only a coincidence; her body was found about eighteen months after my aunt Ellen disappeared. The description could've matched any woman of a similar age. By the time she was pulled from the tree fork, her weathered bones were covered in rags of dried flesh. Who could say for certain what she'd looked like in life?

It was an interesting story, I'd give it that. I wished I'd stumbled across it in my research days, or even as some passing article down an internet rabbit hole. I wished I hadn't seen it at the start of October, when every cub reporter and junior editorial writer wants a good spooky tale to grab the eyeballs of readers in the seasonal spirit.

I could've used more meat, less sizzle.

But prompted by Judith and driven now by curiosity, I called up Google Maps and plugged in "Cinderwich, TN"—a place so bleak and scary-sounding that it absolutely had to be real. There it was, yes. About thirty miles outside of Chattanooga, not terribly far from Nickajack Lake.

I fiddled with the screen, expanding and narrowing my view of the place. It didn't take me long to find the train station. The town had been a stop on the Memphis-Charleston line, back when that meant something. The station was long abandoned, and the visible tracks were hopelessly overgrown. No one had come or gone from Cinderwich by rail in decades.

Then I fiddled around until I found the Rockford Place Inn on what used to be the main drag. It was an old building, colonial revival, or so I'd guess at a glance. It might've been there already in the 1850s when the line was finished, or it might've come along shortly thereafter. Its flat, simple brick façade was a stripped-down version of the form, and its narrow white columns were not quite correct. They'd probably been replaced sometime in the 20th century.

I didn't see anyone on the street. When the little Google car had gone through taking pictures, the town had been a wasteland of boarded windows, dusty doors, and a few parked cars that might've been there temporarily or permanently—it was hard to tell.

I closed my laptop and sat there on the couch, staring into space.

The TV was on, and I'd lost track of what show was playing. Probably an oddball History Channel special about the search for Bigfoot or something on DIY about flipping houses in a city nobody wants to live in. It didn't matter. When I wanted background noise, I didn't want riveting content. I wanted something just interesting enough that it didn't annoy me so I wouldn't have to get up, find the remote, and turn it off.

I heard the word "aliens" and fished around in the couch cushion until I found the remote. I shut it all down with the push of a button.

I sat alone in semi-darkness, staring at the blank black screen.

Judith wanted to meet me in Cinderwich, where the corpse of my aunt Ellen almost certainly was not found in a tree in 1979. But I hadn't seen Judith in several years, and the distance between us had been awkward. I was prepared to blame myself for that part if it would make anything easier. It probably wouldn't.

The truth was, I very badly wanted to see her—now that the

option was on the table. I was also a little afraid to see her, for no good reason at all, simultaneously dreading the prospect and deciding what to wear. What to pack. Should I bring her a gift? Something small that says, "I'm sorry I ghosted you. I'm sorry I'm not the right Ellen. I missed you, and I thought of you, even as I avoided you."

Surely there was some product out there to fit the bill, some blank card that I could add to the top—with something weak and noncommittal, but also warm and gently funny written inside.

"I'm an idiot," I told the room at large.

And it was true, but I hit "reply" anyway.

CHAPTER TWO

JUDITH and I agreed to meet at the hotel at three o'clock.

That way, she'd have plenty of time to land in Chattanooga, rent a car, and make the rest of the drive at her leisure. But by the time my two-hour drive had turned into a three-hour drive—courtesy of some road work—I was pretty confident that she would beat me into town. While trapped in a stop-and-go slog, I shot her a text to say I was running late, but she didn't respond. I figured she was still on the plane, or maybe driving.

Finally, I pulled off at one of those exits that doesn't even have a gas station at the end of the ramp, just a couple of signs that indicate state roads by number. Siri acted like she knew what she was doing, so I let her direct me to the east, and around the bend of the road, I found a gas station after all. I don't know how long it'd been closed and boarded up, but the remaining numbers on the big white sign said that unleaded was $1.12 a gallon.

Ten minutes later, I was well and truly in the middle of nowhere.

The road had two lanes and that was it—sometimes there wasn't even a line in the middle. Trees gone orange or naked lined the way. The scenery was broken up by rusted-out road markers and the occasional tragedy of decomposing roadkill. Leaves blew across the road, dragged that way by a dry, spinning gust. It wasn't raining yet, but I could smell it in the air when I cracked the window.

Moldering leaves, a distant campfire, and rain-to-come: the Appalachian foothills' version of pumpkin spice.

Several miles farther along, the road got a stripe down the middle again, and I started to see cross-streets—or at least turn-offs —where somebody used to live, once upon a time. A set of railroad tracks appeared, and I drove over them; there was nothing to stop me, and it was clear that the tracks were no longer in use. They probably hadn't seen any trains since gas was $1.12 a gallon.

Up ahead, I saw a flashing red light at a four-way stop. Siri said to turn right, so I did, and that's when I got my first good look at the town of Cinderwich.

Or what was left of it.

The internet had prepared me for the emptiness and the Closed signs and the vacant sense of decay. It hadn't prepared me for the quiet.

I didn't see any other vehicles parked in front of the blank store-fronts beside the old parking meters. Every third meter was missing its head, leaving a jagged metal neck to bear witness to the street without cars, without people, without even tumbleweeds.

The next block was a little brighter in that I saw three parked cars—one was definitely not abandoned—and a short, fat white woman walking a small, skinny black dog. At the end of the road, I saw a squared-off roundabout that circled a big stone courthouse. The courthouse entrance was flanked by historic markers, both of which were covered in bird shit. On the town square, every other shop front was empty, but the occupied spots held the sort of thing you'd expect: a small diner, a mom-and-pop grocery, a post office, and somebody-or-another—attorney at law.

I was relieved to see even these small signs of civilization and downright happy to see a normal-looking couple strolling down the sidewalk and laughing. I circled the courthouse and took the left-most exit, pausing to let an older woman cross at the walk, and kept going until I saw a brick neo-colonial with wrong-sized columns at the end of the block.

The sign said, "Rockford Inn, est. 1857". Around back, I found a parking lot with other cars occupying two of the five free spaces. One was a brown Oldsmobile from the eighties, so it surely wasn't

Judith's rental car. The other was a newer Hyundai, so I thought that might've been it.

I pulled my little rolling suitcase off the backseat, locked my vehicle out of habit, and walked around to the front door.

It was huge; easily nine feet tall and as heavy as you'd expect something of that size might be. It was probably solid oak, and it'd been painted a dozen shades of white a dozen times over. Flakes as big as my fingers peeled down low enough to dangle and swipe as I pushed the door and came inside.

The lobby was a little too dark for my comfort, with curtains shading too much of the dirty windows, and lamps that were too small, with bulbs that were too dim.

The furnishings were old enough to call vintage, but not nice enough to call antique. The patterns in the wallpaper clashed gently with the fabric on the couch and loveseats, and the stained-glass panels that hung in the windows were brightly-colored yet covered in dust. They cast muted stripes of candy-colored light across the battered hardwood floors and their threadbare rugs.

A large portrait of a severe Victorian woman in mourning garb was mounted above a great stone fireplace that could've roasted a small car. She clutched a black book and a glass carafe against her chest and stared down at the room with a permanent glare of disapproval. I didn't like her, but the feeling was surely mutual. She had the kind of face that said she'd never liked anything, not even once, not even by accident. If I'd been twenty years younger, I would've flipped her off on principle.

But I'm not twenty years younger, and anyway, a woman was watching me from the front desk. The space was only about as wide as a teacher's desk, with a pegboard behind it that had real, honest-to-God keys hanging from tiny hooks.

The woman said hello and asked if she could help me.

I dragged my rolling suitcase across the lobby and nodded at her, then said, "Yes ma'am, thank you." She probably wasn't ten years older than me, so maybe in her early fifties, but I used ma'am to be on the safe side.

"Checkin' in?" She opened a ledger book rather than a spreadsheet and started scanning it.

"Yes, I'm … I'm meeting an old friend here—Judith Kane? Has she arrived yet?"

She didn't look up. "Nope. We've only got two other folks stayin' right now, and I know 'em both. Is your friend 'sposed to arrive today?"

"Yeah." I checked my watch. "I thought she'd be here by now honestly. But that's all right. I'll just … check-in and go put my stuff away. If that's okay."

The small, thin woman with cropped black hair nodded at the book. "Here she is. I see the reservation. Kane plus one. But she didn't leave a second name."

"Well, it's me. I mean, what are the odds that it's not?"

She eyed me suspiciously like I'd given her ideas. "How should I know? You could be some sort of stalker or somethin', couldn't you?"

"I guess I could. But I'm not," I added fast. "We're coming here because we read an article in the Times-Free Press about—"

She finished my sentence before I could do it myself. "Ellen and the blackgum tree."

"Right." I closed my mouth, feeling like I maybe shouldn't have said anything. Too late now.

"I heard the story ran a week or two ago in the big Chattanooga paper," she said, jotting something in the ledger and closing it. "Swear to God, nothin' else ever did happen here."

"Do you …" I looked around at the door, out the windows. Not that I could see anything except the old furniture and the grim portrait over the fireplace. "… have a newspaper here, in Cinderwich?"

"Nope. Not in years."

"Oh. I'm sorry," I said, just to fill the space.

"Newspaper's one of a million things we ain't got no more, but there's no sense bein' sorry about it. What's your name, honey?" She reached into a drawer I couldn't see and pulled out an index card. She clicked a pen and looked at me expectantly. "I'll just leave a message for Ms. Kane, for when she gets in."

"Right, yeah. I'm Kate Thrush. Like the bird," I said out of reflex because so many people frequently asked.

"Thrush like the bird," she echoed as she scrawled it down. "I'll just leave it in the box here in case I'm not on shift when she comes around. I get off in an hour and then my sister comes in. That's Anne, and she can help you with whatever else you need."

Then she gave me a key to room number three.

Room number three was on the first floor, out of three floors in total. There wasn't an elevator—or if there was, I didn't see it—and the stairs looked a hair too narrow to meet modern codes. I passed them on the left and was glad I didn't have to climb them while wrestling a rolling case, even a small one.

A worn carpet runner had faded until it was nearly the same color as the old yellow oak floors beneath it, but it pointed the way down the hall past a couple of other doors: rooms number one and two. Then on the other side of the hall, room number three.

All the numbers were made of the same cheap, old-fashioned metal. They looked like they belonged on the side of a house in a bad neighborhood.

The 3 on my room's door was crooked. I flicked it with my finger, and it straightened, then tilted again. I unlocked the door and poked my head inside.

I'm not sure what I expected, but the room was basically it. Two beds. Matching bedding in a pattern that was popular when I was in high school. There was a desk with a beige phone on it, a wardrobe with an old CRT television sitting inside it, and a small refrigerator rounded out the highlights.

In the nightstand rested a Gideon Bible and inside the front cover, someone had written in blue ballpoint ink: "This is how I'm going to reorganize my life." Then they'd scribbled out the first ten pages of Genesis so thickly that there were holes in the onionskin paper. Only a few words showed through the vandalism.

I closed the book and put it back in the drawer.

I went to the desk and picked up the phone. A reassuring dial tone hummed in my ear. I put the receiver down and pulled out my cell. Two bars. Three if I held it up to the window.

When I pushed the curtains back, I discovered that the room overlooked an overgrown courtyard. It was long and not very wide, with the rundown remains of a large concrete fountain crumbling under the weight and tension of kudzu. I left the curtains open. I liked the light. It made the place look less tired.

A soft scratching noise startled me.

It stopped before I could figure out where it came from, but then I saw a folded piece of paper sticking out from under the door. Quickly, I opened it and said, "Hello?" to an empty corridor. I looked left, checked right, and didn't see so much as a door swinging shut in the distance to indicate that anyone else had been present at all.

I picked up the note and unfolded it. "'There you are,'" I read aloud. "What?"

I opened the door again. There was still no one out there because of course there wasn't.

"What's this supposed to mean?" I asked the empty hall.

I shut the door again. I held the paper up to the light of the window. The note was handwritten in pencil. Could be anybody's handwriting. On second thought, I wasn't sure how many people's handwriting I would recognize, anyway. My mother's maybe? She was an elementary school teacher, and she always produced the perfect, tidy, rounded letters to prove it. My father had been dead for years. I don't know that I'd ever seen anything but his signature.

Judith's?

Yes, I would've known hers. I'd seen it often enough in the margins of my papers and notes—adding her input, correcting me, or agreeing with me. Usually in green ink, because she thought red looked too harsh.

But this—on the paper in my hand—it could've been anyone's. The paper could've come from anywhere. It was blank and unlined without any letterhead. It was probably torn out of a small journal, or maybe a moleskin. It had that same fragile feel to it, and when I held it up to the sun, I could see a faint halo shine through. I folded it again and tossed it onto the desk, deciding that it must've been meant for someone else.

I thought about leaving a note for Judith but then remembered what century this is. I pulled out my phone and sent a text instead: Made it to the hotel. Checked in. Went to see the sights and maybe find some food. Ping me when you arrive.

I waited a few seconds to see if a bubble full of ellipses would indicate that a reply was forthcoming. No such luck. Her plane must've been delayed. She was surely in the air, or maybe in her rental car. I could think of plenty of reasons that she wouldn't respond right away.

I don't know why I was worried about her. I had no reason to be worried about her. I might've just been worried in general, and she was an easy lightning rod for my anxiety. To be frank with myself, it wasn't the first time.

I picked up my purse and the room key and left the hotel to seek distraction.

CHAPTER THREE

CINDERWICH DIDN'T HAVE a newspaper anymore, but they'd had one—once upon a time—and they still had a tiny library branch. It was open and virtually empty except for an elderly black woman who slowly pushed a rusty metal book cart that sagged under the weight of its cargo. She veritably crept down the aisle, her shaking, bony fingers putting one book here, another book there.

The whole place was only the size of a modest house, but it had a "New Releases" table with a few current bestsellers and a row of computers against one wall. A sign said that the internet password was Shhhhh123, but I hadn't brought my laptop. I sat down at one of the public monitors.

I began by typing "Ellen in the blackgum" into the browser's search bar, but it popped up in full before I even had the first three letters down. I stared at the offerings in the drop-down menu: "ellen in the black gum tree", "ellen in the blackgum tree murder", "who put ellen in the tree", and another half dozen permutations of my inquiry swam to the digital surface.

I stared at the screen so intently that I almost didn't notice the shadow behind me. It was the ancient librarian, grizzled and sharp-eyed, in a polyester dress and black orthopedic shoes.

She looked at my browser and shook her head. "I knew it. That dead woman—she wore a groove in this town. Everyone who visits here, everyone who just passes through … they all fall into her story.

Some of 'em stay there, trapped. Even the folks who get to leave, they always take some part of her with 'em."

I swiveled my seat to look at her instead of her reflection on the screen. "So … who do you think she was?"

She shook her head. "The real question is the one that brought you here: Who do you think she might've been? Your nervous little face says it was someone close." When I didn't answer right away, she continued with a string of guesses. "A dead mother? Long-lost cousin? A lady you saw in an old photo tucked away in your dad's things? Did you find it in a box after he died?"

"Are those … are those some of the theories you've heard before?"

"Those and a hundred more. Now answer my question, if you'd be so kind. Who's she to you?"

I cleared my throat and sat up straight. "I think she might've been my aunt, Ellen Thrush. She went missing in—"

"—1977 or so? No one ever found her body? Seeking closure for your family? Oh, honey," she said and patted my shoulder. The pat wasn't exactly friendly, but it wasn't malicious either. I think it was bored. "'Til the day those little girls found that body in the tree, I swear to God, I had no idea how many young women go missin' in a year. Even very specific young white women with dark blonde or light brown hair goin' by the name of 'Ellen'. You wouldn't think there'd be more than a couple in the whole damn country. But—" and now the slow headshake returned, "you'd be wrong."

She looked like she was about to walk away, but she'd given me an idea. Before she could leave, I asked, "Ma'am, what about the girls who found the body?"

"There were three of 'em. Innocent little things, before that day. What about 'em?"

"Do they still live around here? I wonder if they'd talk to me."

The librarian snorted. "You wonder, and so has everybody else for the last forty years."

I knew I was losing her. "What about … what about the tree itself? Where can I find it?"

"You can't," she told me bluntly. "It was cut down years ago. I'm sorry, but I can't help you. I'm sorry about your aunt." Then she pushed the battered metal cart away, to reload and unload, until the end of time. Or until the next time some fool like me came into her library, sat down at a computer, and began asking the internet questions about who Ellen might have been, and why she'd been found in the blackgum tree in 1979.

I felt stupid, I'll admit. Did I honestly think, via the magic of proximity, that a search engine in Cinderwich might tell me more than the one on my laptop at home? I should've had better sense than to try.

But come to think of it, the desk clerk at the inn had said there used to be a newspaper. The library must have archives of it, the kind of records I couldn't get my hands on in Knoxville or Chattanooga. If I was lucky, I might even find something like microfiche or film—stuff I hadn't played with since grad school. Research Methods of Bibliography, that was the class. Our professor had given us a list of obscure trivia questions, and we had one week to find the answers at the university library. I found all but one, and I felt like an idiot about it until she told the class that the answer was that nobody knew. She'd thrown it in to keep us on our toes.

Those of us who'd discovered the rest felt betrayed. Our fellow students who hadn't given so much of a shit had pointed at us nerds and laughed.

Despite my embarrassment and the sense that I'd wasted a lot of time, I'd enjoyed learning my way around the microfiche. It was so gloriously retro, even decades ago, when I was still studying. So noisy, the spools clicking as the film unfurled. The peculiar plastic and metal smell of the old gears turning and the fizz of the light inside the projector. The frames zooming past at lightning speed … it felt like traveling through time.

I stood up and looked for the librarian, but she was gone. I was ready to chase her down and ask about the archived media when I saw a sign that announced its location. I was ready to try again, knowing full well that the newspapers I wanted from 1979 would probably be the only things anybody had viewed in decades.

But then my purse buzzed. I pulled out my phone and found a text from Judith: Made it to the hotel. Where are you?

Library, I responded. I'll come back and meet you.

No, don't. Meet me at the diner on the main drag. I'm starving.

I remembered passing it on the way in. So, I said, Okay see you there in ten.

I flashed one last longing look at the non-digital media archives. They called to me, or old, weird nostalgia called me. Something did.

But Judith called me too, and I could only answer one of them at a time, so I went back to my car.

I couldn't remember the name of the diner so I couldn't ask Siri to send me there directly, but I had a decent idea of where it was, and I found it in about five minutes. Parking was free and plentiful, so I pulled near the front door in a spot with a broken-necked meter that no one could possibly expect me to feed. I set the emergency brake out of habit, not necessity, and sat there in my seatbelt for another 90 seconds.

Judith was already inside.

I watched her through the window, psychically daring her to look at me. Back in the day, we used to joke about having that kind of connection. She would call me, just when I was thinking about her; I would show up with Chinese takeout when she was hungry, but she hadn't said anything about it yet.

If it'd ever been real, it wasn't anymore.

She never lifted her eyes and never saw me sitting there, watching her like some kind of creep.

I opened the door and tried to get out of the car, then remembered my seatbelt, and tried again. It wasn't my most graceful exit, but the second time was a charm, and my clumsiness had caught Judith's attention whereas my telepathic shout-out had not.

She looked up from what must've been her phone and smiled and waved. She mouthed something, but I didn't catch it. I half pretended to. I smiled back and pointed at the diner's front door like a dumbass, because where the hell else would I go.

The sign above the door said the place was called simply, "The Depot", and its furnishings were less retro-hip than raggedy. The floors were scuffed vinyl, and the counters were rimmed with chrome that had worn off around the elbows of patrons for decades. The barstools were split and ripped, bleeding yellow foam.

I noticed all of these things and a million more, for the world was moving in slow motion as Judith rose from her seat and opened her arms to greet me.

I had missed her. I had not missed her. I don't know how I'd been feeling all this time except that there'd been a hole in my life where she used to be. A wound, maybe. Something that never really closed.

She was lovely still. Her hair was more silver than the salt-and-pepper I'd seen it last, and her eyes were that odd shade of brown that was nearly gold—even more striking now with the short, sharp pixie haircut. Judith was slim, as always, and likewise graceful. Gold charm bracelets chimed on her right wrist and a digital fitness tracker blinked on the left.

I fell into the offered hug and squeezed her in return. She was strong against me, and she smelled like a single-note perfume. Violets today. Sometimes it was roses, sometimes jasmine. She'd toyed with lilac once, but as I recall she didn't care for it.

"What?" she asked me. Something about the look on my face I guess.

"The perfume. You and your lonely flowers."

She smiled and crow's feet blossomed at the edges of her eyebrows. It made my heart hurt and I can't explain why. I'm sure I looked older to her too, but I doubt it bothered her any.

"This is a year of violets," she told me, releasing me from the hug and holding me at arm's length just to look at me. "Violets and arrows, though I couldn't say why." She always had a theme, every year. Now that she'd named it for me, I noticed the tiny gold arrow studs in her ears and the arrowhead charm on one of the bangles.

"I like it," I told her. It sounded tight; the sentiment squeezed through my teeth. I couldn't stop smiling. "You look amazing."

"As do you." She patted my shoulders and let me sit down. "I'm so glad you could make it; you have no idea."

I scooted into the booth across from her, my jeans snagging briefly on a long, sharp tear in the seat. "I'm so glad you emailed. You have no idea," I parroted her and laughed awkwardly. "I just … I have some downtime between classes right now. You couldn't have picked a better week to propose this adventure."

The waitress chose that moment to wander over and ask what I wanted to drink.

"I already ordered," Judith said. "I hope you don't mind."

"Not at all." I scanned the menu. It had already been sitting on the table, like a paper placemat. I went for the easy order. "I'll have a diet soda and ... and a cheeseburger. With fries. And extra ketchup."

"Some things never change."

"Ketchup is fucking delicious," I solemnly informed her for what must've been the millionth time.

We spent a good half an hour on small talk and catching up, falling into the old patterns that had been both comforting and stifling—or that's how I remembered it. But I didn't feel stifled just then; I mostly felt an embarrassing sense of giddy pleasure to be in her presence. I found myself teetering toward the familiar approval-seeking, the old teacher/student arrangement that was always both too much and not enough.

I don't know if Judith felt it too—the reassuring return to a routine—but she certainly filled the role effortlessly. I couldn't tell whether I was relieved or unsettled. A little of each? Something else entirely? Maybe it didn't have a name.

When we were finished with our food and running out of chit-chat and the straggling remainders of fries lay cooling on our plates, we retreated to the only safe subject we'd ever had between us: the first Ellen Thrush and the mystery thereof.

"How long have you been here?" she asked me.

"Oh, I only beat you by an hour or so. I haven't had time to learn anything new."

"I do apologize for the delay. There was so much traffic," she explained, leaning back in the booth and sprawling out with one arm on the back of the seat and the other settling on the windowsill. "But boy, that hotel is something else, isn't it? Ellen would've loved it. She was always a secret goth at heart."

"None more southern gothic than the Rockford," I agreed. "None more creepy either." I almost mentioned the note I'd found under the door but didn't. It was probably an accident, meant for someone else. It wasn't worth sharing.

"You said you were at the library when I texted?"

I nodded. "Always a good place to start."

"Always. Did you learn anything good?"

"Mostly that we're late to the party. Everybody and their brother has been through Cinderwich looking for Ellen and the blackgum tree."

She shrugged and picked at a fry. "Ellen put them on the map."

Diplomatically, I said, "There's not much else to talk about around here. Everything is pretty much … gone, as far as I can tell. They used to have a newspaper. Used to have parking meters," I said, cocking my thumb at my spot on the other side of the window. "Used to have more than one restaurant probably. I hear they used to have a lot of things."

"But they've still got a library, and that's the important part. Does it have microfilm, or fiche, or anything along those lines?"

"It does. I was about to check it out when you pinged me. "

"Good," she nodded. "I've done all the digging I can on the internet. Now we need boots on the ground. I figure we can start with the girls who found the body in 1979."

"Great minds think alike, eh? I asked about them, but the librarian gave me the distinct impression that they don't talk to anyone. Hell," I mumbled. "If I found a corpse in a tree when I was a kid, I wouldn't want to spend the next forty years talking about it either."

"No, but that won't stop me from trying to get them on the record anyway. I've tracked down the three of them and it was easier than I thought. It's too bad the other two are dead."

I frowned at her and picked at one of my orphaned fries. I still had a puddle of ketchup that needed pillaging. "Other two?"

"The mystery woman was found by a party of five, but somewhat curiously, two of the girls drowned. One died just a year later in 1980. One died a little after that, in 1984. The other three are still local." She stuffed the nubbin of cooled potato into her mouth, chewed it, and swallowed.

The waitress manifested at our table as if summoned by a circle. She slipped us our bill and asked with careful indifference, "You talkin' about Ellen and the tree?"

Judith was faster than me. "Oh yes. Fascinating story isn't it?"

She made a little noise like, "eh." Then she said, "Sure, if you've only heard it a thousand times. Don't get me wrong, I feel sorry for her, and I feel sorry for the ladies who found her, and sorry for anybody who … who lost somebody and never found her. But she's old news around here. I don't mean to sound rude," she concluded somewhat sheepishly. "She's all anybody wants to talk about. That, and sometimes the railroad men and the Freemasons."

I opened my mouth to ask what she meant. All I managed was "Freemasons?"

"Yeah, but that's old news too. Sorry. Didn't mean to interrupt."

Judith nodded with sympathy. "No, no. And thank you for chiming into the conversation. I suppose you must've heard about Ellen and the blackgum tree from every angle, every nuance. Over and over again."

The young woman's head bobbed. "God, yes. I wasn't born here, but I've been here long enough to know all about her."

She raised an eyebrow. "All about her? Then perhaps you could tell us about the ladies you just mentioned."

"The ladies … you know. The girls who found the body. They grew up, like people do." She wiped her hands on a towel that was hanging out of her apron pocket. "It's funny, how they turned out. They never exactly left, but nobody hardly ever sees them. They're spooky as hell, all three of them."

"How so?" Judith asked. I was still wondering what was up with the Freemasons, but whatever. The chatter had moved along without me, so I let it drop.

Our server waved her hand vaguely. "Oh, you know. Just creepy old ladies. They don't really talk to anyone except each other. Maybe they all still live together in that big, stupid house, I don't know. The youngest one—sometimes she leaves. I don't know where she goes."

I said, "Well, they shared a rather tremendous … experience. And do you mind if I ask? What did you mean about the railway-men? Why do people come here asking about them?"

"Oh, just the Barlows and their friends I guess. They had some weird ceremony down at the river."

Judith caught the word and repeated it. "Ceremony?"

"Um, I think it was more like a festival or somethin'. I don't know. Maybe a party. Somethin' about the water." She shrugged, and it didn't mean anything. "Anyhow, here's your check. Bring it up to the register when you're ready."

When she was gone, Judith and I stared at each other—unsure of whether we should laugh or immediately run out and find those three "creepy old ladies". They couldn't be that old. They were still kids when I was born. "I still want to know what's up with the whole railway ceremony thing. That sounds weird."

"It's definitely weird, and it rings a bell. Let's pay up and go back to the hotel," she suggested. "It's too late for a social call, and I want to send off an email or two."

We each stopped at the register and retreated to our cars, then parked beside one another at the Rockford Inn. Back around to the front we went, and through the oversized doors, into the lobby.

A different woman was at the counter. Anne, I assumed.

Judith and I both made polite murmurs of greeting, and my companion headed back toward the room, but I hesitated—caught in the gravitational field of that crazy painting over the fireplace mantle. Judith realized she'd lost me and stopped. "Quite a portrait isn't it?" she observed.

"It's like … she hates me. Me, personally."

"Now that's hardly fair," said the desk clerk with a gently reproachful air that said I'd spoken out of turn. "Miss Barlow had a difficult life, and perhaps it shows in the paint. There's nothin' hateful about her, not at all."

"If you say so."

Judith returned to my side, partly to see the painting better and partly to reclaim me, I think. "Victoria Barlow—wasn't that her name?" she asked Anne.

"Yes! How did you know?"

"My magical research powers," she said to me with a wink. Then to the clerk, she added, "I always do my homework before I travel." On the way to our room, she elaborated. "The Barlows built this town, more or less. Richard was a freemason and a minor railroad bigwig—"

"So more like a middlingwig?"

"Fine, if you like." She pulled out her key and opened the door. "A middlingwig. If he'd been a bigger wig, he would've no doubt built his family estate in Nashville or even Chattanooga. But he built this hotel, and he used to own most of the town."

"Some men would rather have a fief than a mere estate."

"Indeed. He and his wife had two daughters, Victoria and

Meredith. Neither one ever married, nor had any children. Alas, for poor Mr. Barlow, his line died out accordingly."

I glanced down at the floor to see if there were any fresh notes slipped inside while we were away. I didn't see anything. "Two sisters? How come there's only one woman in the painting?"

Judith flopped on the bed farthest from the door and closest to the large window that overlooked the tiny courtyard. "Oh, the usual nineteenth-century family tragedy. Meredith went mad, or so it was generally agreed. She was briefly institutionalized but came home to kill herself. Poor dear was only about your age when she died. I'm sure she's somewhere in the little cemetery near the station, but I couldn't find any proof of it. She was buried quietly, without any fanfare."

"Not even a stone?"

"Google Street View couldn't help me out with that one. Maybe we'll look her up later. Pay our respects, or whatever." She didn't sound like she meant it, but it could be hard to tell. Exhuming dead madwomen of old used to be her favorite pastime. But I was out of practice when it came to Judith Kane. Meredith wasn't the mission.

I tried shifting the subject back to Ellen. "Any chance the street view showed you any spooky graffiti? Shit, we should've asked the waitress about it."

"The Chattanooga article said the most recent round was applied to the train station, and I believe it's still there." She reached for her purse and dug around in its assorted pockets. "Didn't need the waitress for that one, bless her heart. But it was strange wasn't it? That whole conversation."

"No stranger than the one I had at the library. The whole town is sick of Ellen. I get the feeling Cinderwich would prefer that she'd never happened." I was remembering the librarian and the odd way she'd put it: She wore a groove into this town.

Drolly, Judith said, "If Ellen hadn't happened, Cinderwich would be completely abandoned by now. She's the only tourist attraction they've got." She retrieved her cell phone, pulled up her pictures, and said, "Come here, see? I found a hard copy of the paper, and there was a picture. I took a—well, a picture of the picture. I don't know why it wasn't online."

She held up her phone and I took it in my hands, holding it up and horizontally so the photo would expand to its full size. There it was, on the side of a building: "Who put Ellen in the blackgum tree?"

The handwriting shocked me, but I tried not to let it show.

I'd seen it before, on a note slipped under a door when no one was around. I told myself that I was mistaken and I didn't believe me, but I had to keep talking. "Do you … do you think the color means something? What is that? Yellow spray paint?"

"Yellow is often the color of remembrance. It could symbolize loss? It also represents caution, as often as not. Then again, there could have been a sale on yellow at the local Ace Hardware. Not everything needs to be profound."

"Surely the paint wouldn't have been bought around here," I protested. "If somebody local bought yellow spray paint, and then yellow graffiti turned up, everyone would know who did it."

"Maybe everybody does know."

"That's just crazy talk."

She laughed at me, not with me. "You say that like you've never been to a small town before. Towns keep secrets for their own. Just like families do."

"And lovers." It wasn't a necessary addendum, and I don't think she appreciated it. I told myself that I didn't care.

She paused, then continued like she hadn't heard me. "Insular groups of all kinds and all numbers, they'll protect their own if they think they need to. It's a very human instinct. But we'd better hope that's not what's happening here. If the truth about Ellen and the graffiti is a town-wide secret, you can safely bet that no one will open up to us about it."

I handed Judith her phone back and said, "That's why we need a good, old-fashioned paper trail. Documents or pictures that have been filed away, or lost, or hidden. Our specialty, right? Between the pair of us, we'd make a killer set of history detectives."

She smiled warmly. "Absolutely. If we can't find it, it doesn't exist." Then the smile waned. "If it doesn't exist, then we've hit another dead end."

I sat on the edge of my bed, facing her. "Don't say that. We haven't even started yet. Don't doom us to failure before we can find our footing."

"You're right. I'm being a pessimist, and a pessimist's prophecies are always self-fulfilling. Let's assume the best, shall we? Tomorrow we'll go see the graffiti—at least, see if it's still there—and I have an address for the women who found the corpse as girls. Hard to say if they'll be home, or if anyone will be willing to talk, or even if my information is any good. But it's a place to start."

"I'll take it," I said. Then I reached into my bag and pulled out a bottle of Bulleit's rye and a couple of folding plastic cups.

"It's a little early for that, don't you think?"

"Nah," I argued. "It's almost dark, and there's nothing else we can do tonight. May as well turn on the TV and have a drink. Here …" I put the cups and the bottle on the nightstand between our two beds. "Help yourself. I'm going to take a shower and settle in."

CHAPTER FOUR

I SHOT AWAKE a little before dawn like drunks always do—thirsty, confused, and ready to fight whatever had disturbed me. But when I opened my eyes, prepared to confront any real or imagined nightmares, I saw only the faint outline of a lamp on the ceiling and the spotty red flash of the smoke detector light.

I sat up and looked around, letting my eyes adjust and my heart rate settle down.

A thin line of sharp, pale light peeked under the main door, and a softer yellow nightlight glow crept around the bathroom door. A vivid blue-white from a security light outside winked around the curtains.

Judith was lying on her back, tucked in so tidily that she looked like an advertisement for a sedative. Her hands were folded across her chest, resting on the perfect fold of the gently tacky bedspread. She wore a black foam eye mask. Somehow, it didn't disturb her hair. She did not snore, and she did not sleep-whistle through her nose.

Meanwhile, I could feel my hair going wild because I'd gone to bed fresh from the shower before it was dry. A crust of drool had formed at the corner of my mouth, one of my eyes was half-gummed shut, and one tit was hanging out of the too-big tank top I should've thrown away years ago.

I tucked my boob back in. I wiped the drool from my mouth and the gunk from my eye. I picked up my glasses from the nightstand and put them on. I didn't often wear them, but I couldn't sleep in my contacts anymore, so I had to keep them on hand. Getting older really is hell in a million small and inconvenient ways, never mind the large ones.

I could hear something now. I couldn't put my finger on what it was, except that it was coming from rather far away, and the noise was almost certainly what had awakened me.

I swung my feet over the side of the bed and felt around for my flip-flops. It may have been early fall, but it was plenty warm enough for sandals, and I've always hated walking around public spaces (like hotel rooms) while barefoot. Finding them, I wormed my toes into place and stood. One of my knees popped loudly enough to make me jump, but Judith didn't budge.

Now. What the hell was that noise?

A push, a scrape, a thud. Three sounds then. Working together as one. I crept to the door, checking the bottom again for messages. Nothing, except that the odd sound was louder there. I put my ear to the door and listened.

I looked back at Judith, perfection in slumber, and picked up my room key from on top of my closed suitcase. I squeezed it in my palm to keep it from jingling. Carefully, I slipped out, letting the door shut softly behind me. I barely heard the click the knob made.

Push, scrape, thud.

It echoed off the walls of the narrow corridor, bouncing off the doors in some trick of acoustics.

I squinted one way, then the other, and realized that I wasn't alone in the corridor. I only saw her for an instant—a pale woman with wild black hair, wearing a light gray dress or nightgown. She turned on her heel the moment I spotted her and ducked around the corner with the big red EXIT sign.

The noise went with her.

"Hello?" I shout-whispered to the last hint of her shadow before it vanished.

I trailed behind her, for no real reason apart from curiosity. I wasn't afraid. It was only a woman. For all I knew, she was looking for a vending machine. She might have been sleepwalking.

"Hello?" I tried again.

Her footsteps retreated and I followed them. I passed the EXIT sign and saw that same flash—an ombre moment of black medusa curls, swirling gray fabric, and naked white feet.

I didn't call out again. Either she couldn't hear me or she wasn't listening. I just followed in her wake, glimpsing those light feet, that dark hair, every time I rounded one corner and she rounded the next.

I became dizzy, I'm not sure when. I'm not sure how.

There were so many corners—more than the little hotel could've possibly accommodated. Were we going in circles? Was I getting lost in this small, dark place with only a dozen rooms for rent? How? The sound was getting louder, so it couldn't be a wild goose chase. I couldn't have been going in circles, because I was clearly getting closer to the source.

Ahead, I heard a door open and the push, scrape, thud rose in volume.

The woman hadn't shut the door behind herself, and although a warning on the handle said "ALARM WILL SOUND", no alarm had, in fact, sounded. The door swung outward on its hinges, creaking and drifting in a breeze that was just strong enough to tug it.

Push, scrape, thud.

I shoved the door far enough to let myself out and stood in the overgrown courtyard I'd seen through my own room's window. I was very confused. I knew I'd taken too many turns to be right back here, but it was late—or early—and I was not at my personal sharpest. I looked left, looked right, and scanned the scene for the woman in gray, but I didn't spot her.

The sound, though.

It was clear as a bell out there in the night, where the air was thick because rain was rolling in. Thin clouds coated the stars like a scummy film, and the little town smelled like early fall. It smelled like the river too, or I thought it did. The river was a mile or more away, and the big lake was much farther away than that, so it had to be my imagination. Besides, the river didn't usually smell like wet things rotting, not this late in the year. Down by the dams in the middle of summer, yes; they'd stink of hot dead fish and whatever the big chemical plant was still spewing into the ecosystem. But not in Cinderwich. Cinderwich should smell like coal dust and railroad timbers with a hint of mildew and fried food.

I don't know why I thought that. I don't know why I kept looking around the courtyard with its strangled fountain and feeble security lamp that gave it a cold, half-assed light.

I was drawn to the creepy rhythm of that three-part sound, desperately trying to place it. From time to time, the pattern was interrupted by the quick ping of metal on rocks. Yes, that's what the interloping chime was: the sharp noise of steel on stone.

Out past the edge of the courtyard, I tracked it, my flip-flops sliding around on my feet. Dew was already collecting on the grass, and my toes struggled to hang onto the cheap shoes; I crunched my feet into fists to lock them down and soldiered on.

There she was. At the far side of the parking lot behind the courtyard.

I stopped. I had no flashlight, and I stood at the edge of the very last glimmers of electric glow from the security lamp and the street-lamps on the other side of the building.

But the woman was looking at me. I could see her in bits and pieces, in shadows half-cast by the trees. She was small and lovely with large, bright eyes. Enough wavy, dark hair to stuff a pillow swarmed her face and fell to her hips. She did not blink. She did not breathe. Her snow-white feet did not quite touch the ground.

I didn't gasp or cry out.

She couldn't be floating above the asphalt, beside the woods. I could see her with my own two eyes, and that meant she was at least as real as I was. My brain wouldn't allow her to be anything except a tiny, beautiful, peculiarly monstrous thing. Flesh and blood. Long hands with fingers like talons—it was something about the way she held them, slightly curled, one at her side and one at her chest. Long hair that moved, even when she did not. Even when the air did not.

I shivered and hugged myself. We had only a little stretch of pavement between us, and this strange string of noises repeating over and over again, so loudly that I could hardly concentrate on anything else.

Except for her.

"Hello?"

She replied with a nod, not quite returning the greeting, but admitting that she'd heard it.

"What are we doing out here?"

Silently, she raised one long, white arm from which hung a sleeve that was ragged with old lace. She pointed toward the woods behind her and then held that same pointing finger to her lips, telling me to be quiet.

"Okay," I whispered. "What's back there?"

Her eyebrows knitted together. She pressed her finger to her mouth again.

"Sorry!" I whispered even more quietly. Then I just mouthed the word: Sorry.

I was shaking. I must have been afraid, I must have been cold. I couldn't really tell; everything was numb. I couldn't feel my toes, locked into my flip-flops. I couldn't feel my hands, though they were squeezing my arms as I hugged myself.

It must have been colder than I thought. She must have been dead.

I started walking, one unfeeling foot after another, in the direction she'd shown me. I didn't want to leave the last of the light. I was walking away from it and I couldn't stand the thought of it, but I couldn't stop myself either. She might have been drawing me forward. She might have only been watching.

I came close enough to touch her, or close enough to try. If I'd put out my hand to brush hers, would I have met any resistance? Would my skin have passed through hers, like light through a window?

Would she have been cold? Would she have cared?

I didn't do it. I thought about it, but I was distracted by a shimmer of something dull but alight, back in the trees, maybe twenty yards away. Someone had left a lantern sitting on a stump.

I let go of the ghost, or I quit looking at her. I focused on the lantern with its watery white light. Soon I could hear the hiss of propane behind the infernal push, scrape, thud. A person-shaped shadow moved in a clearing, its motions obscured by the tree trunks until I was near enough that I felt I ought to hide.

I chose a large tree and tried to make myself small behind it. My cheap foam shoes slid around on the tree roots and slipped on the grass. I kicked them off and stuck my left middle finger through the loops where my big toes ought to go so I wouldn't lose them. The ground was chilly and hard.

I clutched my arms again.

Someone was swinging, up and down. Again and again.

Someone was wearing overalls, a flannel, and work boots. Someone was a woman, I realized; her hair was tied up in a scarf, and there was something about her posture, the way she moved her arms. The way she stood when she paused to take a break.

She was facing away from me. She leaned on a shovel, wiped her forehead with the back of her arm, and then stepped down into a hole that was maybe knee-deep.

Beside me, so close I should've felt her breath on my shoulder, the lady in gray appeared.

I froze. What else could I do? She was there at my side, so close I could have kissed her if I could have caught her. She was so small and so perfect with a look in her eyes that was madness and certainty and more than a hint of rage.

I tried to remember to breathe.

I watched the woman dig. Was she burying something?

The ghost shook her head.

Was she looking for something?

The ghost twisted her lips. My unspoken guess was closer, but she wasn't giving me a "yes." Then finally, she spoke. I heard her words as if they came from the other end of the world and only the barest hints of their shape reached my ear.

We have to let it out.

I almost asked, "Let what out?" but when I blinked, she was gone. Nothing was left of her except a sense that the air was a little colder in that one place and the shadows were very dull again in her absence.

For one stupid second, I considered just saying hello to the woman in the clearing and asking what the midnight excavation was all about, but I came to my senses in time to sneak back to the hotel parking lot. It was none of my business. It could've been something private—burying a deceased pet, or digging for family heirlooms buried a generation before.

Anyway, the woman was bigger than me and she had a shovel. I didn't want to piss her off.

I returned, barefoot and breathing too hard, to the hotel's back door. I remembered my flip-flops dangling from my hand. I dropped them on the ground and put them on, feeling a fresh layer of grit between my skin and the foam sole. I put my hand on the knob and it was frigid, so bitterly icy that I thought my fingers would freeze there if I tried to let it go.

By reflex, I jerked away. It was nonsense, or a mistake. My hand was fine. The doorknob was the same bland temperature as the air around me.

I twisted it with a yank and stumbled back inside.

The corridor was blank and bright after the darkness outside. It was disorienting. I'd followed the ghost around corner after corner after corner, but my room was only one turn away. I tried not to think too hard about it. I thought too hard about it anyway, as I fumbled with my key and then fumbled with everything else as I tried to crawl back into bed in silence.

Judith had rolled over in her sleep and now she faced the window. That made it easier.

I made a point to not look at the clock. I didn't want to know what time it was. I wanted to go back to sleep and pretend I'd never left the room, but that wasn't how it worked. Instead, I kicked the blankets around and wiggled every joint, trying to get comfortable. But comfortable never happened.

CHAPTER FIVE

JUDITH and I drove out to the interstate to get breakfast. There was a Waffle House by the closest exit only a few miles out, and our options were limited in town. I wanted food that tasted like it came from civilization, but as we sat in the yellow and brown restaurant, staring out a window at an interstate and the edge of a vast lake, I considered how far my standards for civilization had slipped.

Only a few other customers occupied the place: a couple of truck drivers, a guy who looked like he might've been homeless, and two older women who were giggling over a map.

Judith ate her hash browns with a knife and fork, like the queen of fucking England. I shoveled in a mouthful without any of her cautious ceremony and grinned at her. "Sorry, we couldn't find anything more proper. Something with cloth napkins and ambience."

"Don't be silly. Waffle House is fine. I'm a fan, really."

"Since when?"

"Since ages ago," she said vaguely. "Do you want to know why? I'll tell you if you do."

I could have guessed, but maybe she wanted to talk about it. "Sure. Hit me."

She took another bite before she answered and chewed it so slowly that I thought she must have regretted her offer to tell me anything. But then she said, "Back when Ellen and I were living

together, there was a Waffle House less than a mile away. It wasn't
the best part of town—not the worst either, we just didn't have a lot
of variety. And we were broke, of course. I was new to the assistant
professor gig, hustling to pick up freelance editing jobs on the side.
Ellen was working at an elementary school as a teacher's assistant.
We weren't starving to death, but we couldn't afford a bigger place
in a better neighborhood." She paused and took a sip from her Diet
Coke.

"I thought she was still in school for a while after you two got
together. After you left that, um, gig where you met."

"She dropped out a few weeks after we were outed by my reader
—that little shit. Sharon was her name, I remember. She was only
supposed to grade papers, nothing else was any business of hers,
but she's the one who filed the complaint with Vanderbilt." Judith
was staring through me now. Past me, even.

"What a bitch."

"It would've taken months for the whole thing to cycle through
the administration, but I already knew they were going to fire me;
Ellen probably would've been kicked out of the program if she
hadn't withdrawn. Best case scenario, they would've assigned her to
another advisor or allowed her to transfer to another school …"

"I thought she just dropped out."

She shook her head and fiddled with her plastic cup. "I don't
remember the particulars anymore—only that she left and she
didn't go back. I think she might've eventually taken another swing
at it if we'd had more time. We could've moved again. She could've
joined another program."

"But you didn't have more time." They'd only been together for
a little longer than a year when Ellen vanished.

"I don't know. Yes, I do—there was time to start again fresh,
whether or not there was time to finish anything. But our priorities
had shifted." She didn't sound very certain. "It's a shame though.
Her research was fascinating, and it kills me that it never went
anywhere."

"Unless it brought her here." I put my fork down. I was as full as
I was going to get. "Lady wizards in the middle of nowhere—wasn't
that the gist?"

Judith gave me a look. "Women's medicine as practical magic in rural Appalachia. She was particularly interested in clootie wells and coin trees and things like that. Old-world traditions that made it across the Atlantic. And yes, the possibility that Ellen might've come here for exactly that purpose, it … it did not escape me."

Clootie wells. I hadn't thought of those in years. Was the woman in the woods digging such a thing? They were often set near trees, weren't they? Healing waters in the woods where trees were strewn with ribbons and rags. No, it was too much of a stretch to say it out loud.

I sighed instead. "Well, this definitely qualifies as rural Appalachia. She wasn't still working on that thesis, was she? After she left the program? She wouldn't still be chasing down research leads."

"No. I mean, maybe. I can't say one way or the other to be honest. She was still interested in the subject matter, and she still kept a hanging file box on the top of the closet. Now and again, she would add a new clipping to it or haul it out to put some new notes in there. I think, in the back of her head, she always thought she'd get back to it eventually."

"Yeah, a lot of grad students say that."

"Oh, shut up," she said crossly.

It stung a little. "What? They do. I did; I dropped the post-grad and I never got back to it. That's all I meant."

She picked up her glass and took another sip, and that meant she didn't believe me. She often punctuated her thoughts by taking a drink, taking a puff of a cigarette, taking a bite of a snack. If she'd believed me, she would've just said so, instead of making her opinion part of the performance. "You've spent a lifetime in the shadow of that comparison. She must've been a lot to live up to."

"Or to live down to, depending on who you asked." Before she could become more annoyed with me, I walked it back. "You know how my mom and grandma could get. They never forgave her, and they passed the grudge down to me."

"That wasn't fair of them." Good, I'd successfully redirected her. Never would she admit that she hated my mother, but it always warmed her when I hinted that I did. "They were never fair to either one of you."

"Tell me about it."

"If it makes a difference, you never did look anything like her. Did they tell you that?"

"I saw it for myself in your pictures." But not in my family's pictures of the first Ellen. I don't know if they even had any. If it'd been up to my family, I would have never seen her, only heard of her, and been compared to her, forever and ever. The image in my imagination could never compare to any mere image anyway, so the photos Judith kept in a shoebox might as well be someone else entirely.

Except, of course, they weren't.

Not in my imagination, but in real life, the first Ellen was a little shorter and a little thicker than me. I've always been the tall and skinny type; she was a tad curvy. Her hair was so wavy that you'd almost call it curly. Mine's straight and fine and a few shades lighter. In our cheekbones, in the height of our brows, there was probably some hint of the family resemblance—or at least, you wouldn't call me a liar if I said we were cousins. But that was as far as any resemblance went.

Judith said, "You look even less like her now. The older you get."

"No shit." I changed my mind about the food and took another stab at the last triangle of toast. "I'm almost twenty years older than she was when she—" I almost said died, but caught myself— "went missing." Then I stuffed my mouth so I couldn't say anything else to make the morning more awkward.

Softly, Judith agreed. "That's true. I hadn't thought of it quite like that, but you're right. Enough time has passed, and enough distance … well. She would've been twenty-three the last time I saw her. She was about to be twenty-four. I'd already picked out a couple of birthday presents and even purchased one of them. Never got a chance to give them to her. Now, I suppose, she'd be … late sixties? Maybe seventy? Rumors to the contrary, she wasn't that much younger than me. Not even seven years. What's the joke? The minimum dating coefficient? Half your age plus seven, that's how I heard it—and she easily cleared it, thank you very much."

"I'm sorry. I didn't mean to—"

"It's fine, it's fine. I didn't mean to make it into a thing. Christ, every time you think some old scrape has scabbed over," she complained quietly, mostly to herself. "Let's go. Let's pay up and get down to business."

The cheap diner-style napkins were undersized, even when unfolded. She'd used half a dozen of them to create a splashguard in her lap. Now she wadded them up into a giant ball and put them by her plate.

I almost asked the question I hadn't really asked yet, even though it was the most obvious question in the world: Do you really think this cryptic, hypothetical Ellen was our Ellen? But I didn't. I didn't have an opinion of my own yet. I didn't honestly think we'd ever find neither hide nor hair of my wayward aunt, but if Judith wanted to go wild goose chasing then …

… then what? Then I was on board for it, even after all this time? All this baggage?

Obviously, the answer was yes. Both answers. All the answers, even. If there was no chance—no hope, no belief—then there was no point, and we ought to just pack it up and go home. But here we were instead. At a Waffle House, on the edge of Nickajack Lake, in the Middle of Nowhere, Tennessee.

"Okay," I said, reaching for my purse. "What's our first stop?"

"First, we check the graffiti. It's on one of those buildings down by the train station. Then we look for the tree where they found the body. After that, we look up the girls. We can do all that in a day, I bet."

"The tree was cut down. That's what the librarian said."

She picked up her purse and scooted out of the booth. "No, that's not true. The tree is off the beaten track, but it's still standing, as of a month ago. There's an old fire road that heads out of town. The tree is a mile or two down that path and a little to the east."

"According to who? Some nut on the internet?"

"Some savvy trespasser who posted his results on the internet for nosy people like me."

I didn't like it, and once we were back in the car, I told her so. I was driving, so I felt like I had some measure of authority. I took advantage of it while I could. "Even if we find this tree you located via the internet, there's no guarantee it's the right tree. It could be any goddamn tree."

"It's the right tree."

"Okay, but why do we care, Judith? Seriously. This is supposed to be a fact-finding mission, not a sight-seeing mission. But you want to see the tree, and you want to see the graffiti, like either of them will tell us anything. It's a waste of time."

She crossed her arms and pretended to adjust her seatbelt. "It won't hurt anything to look, and it won't take very much time. You used to be more curious than this."

"Ten years of adjunct teaching has beaten the curiosity right out of me."

"You never settled down in a school? I thought you were at UT."

I nodded toward the windshield and pulled onto the small road that would return us to Cinderwich. "I am. I'm also at the community college out by the River Walk. I juggle the two, so I can make rent."

"Jesus."

"Yeah, I know. But here in the real world, I'm just one more disposable MA who can teach freshman comp. If I went back and got my doctorate, I'd add so much debt that I'd never retire—not at my age. The odds are already against it. Why guarantee it?"

"It's not that bad out there," she argued weakly.

"Yeah, it is. I'm broke, but I've got a small IRA that I add to whenever I get lucky and publish an article or something. I'm too old to start over again," I hit the bottom line. "And I'm too old to sleep my way up to the middle too."

"Don't be ridiculous. The men in charge of your average English department are old enough to be your father," she teased. "I'm sure you could find one or two to give you a leg up."

"Maybe if I had bigger tits," I mused.

"You're terrible."

I grinned. "You love it. Now let's go find ourselves a fire road, whatever the hell that is. Maybe we'll find a tree at the end of it."

She smiled to herself and looked out the window. "Won't that be nice? Yes, I think so." Her breath fogged the window beside her mouth. "Maybe we'll even find a clootie well beside it. Maybe we'll leave ribbons of our own and have our fondest wishes granted."

"Not gonna hold my breath."

She shrugged. "It's probably best that you don't."

CHAPTER SIX

BEFORE LONG, Judith and I were back in the nebulous region that was loosely called Cinderwich, out past the town square. I turned Siri back on because I wasn't terribly confident there in the middling places where the roads had no more than two lanes and half the street signs were toppled and rusted, hidden by the grass. So I followed the digital lady's directions and turned onto a road-like path that used to be paved, but mostly wasn't anymore. Chunks of asphalt remained like stepping stones in a stream of clay and packed dirt, and I drove over them with my teeth clenched for every dip, drop, and bump.

But we reached the train station in one piece and pulled up alongside it to park in an empty lot that was in no better shape than the road that took us to it.

We sat in the car for a minute, getting our purses and phones together so we could take pictures and have Mace ready in case of emergency, like the paranoid old biddies we were. Maybe it was nuts, but we were two women alone in the boonies. We hadn't survived this long by taking stupid chances. Even in lieu of hobo ghosts and axe murderers, there were always coyotes and bears to consider.

Except for the road leading up to it and the grass-clogged tracks alongside it, the train station was practically in the middle of the woods. Nature had overtaken the once bustling place, though it couldn't have bustled that wildly, even in its heyday. The building wasn't any bigger than our hotel, but it was only a single story, so it looked longer and flatter. The remains of a smallish clock tower jutted skyward, burned and blackened.

Judith adjusted her sunglasses and climbed out of the car. She pointed at the tower. "Lightning strike, I bet."

I agreed because it was easy. "Sure, why not."

Many of the windows were covered with plywood and many of the rest were broken. A chain swung loosely between two side doors at a loading dock, and a tree was growing out of one wall, its roots zigzagging around loose bricks and its branches pushing past an old drainpipe to reach for the sun.

"Maybe there's a way inside, around back."

She frowned at me. "Why would we want to get inside?"

"Because … we're here? Don't you think it'd be cool?"

"Not particularly."

"You were just lamenting my lost curiosity," I reminded her. "What about you? Where's your sense of adventure?"

"I'm burning through my annual supply just by being here, Kate. Let's see if we can find the graffiti and get a few pics. Maybe … take some samples, I don't know."

She started walking. I shut my car door and followed her. "Samples of what? For whom?"

"Let's play it by ear."

"Okay, but if my ear sees an open door, I'm turning on my flashlight app and heading inside. You'll just have to wait for me. Or join me."

She kept walking. "Oh, to be so young again."

I fell in line behind her then caught up as we rounded the corner. "Call me a 'whippersnapper' and I'll …"

We both stopped and stood on a little concrete landing outside the station's rear landing. "You'll what?" Judith asked, but she wasn't looking at me. She was looking at the wall in front of us.

I shrugged, but she didn't see it. "I'll commence with further empty threats."

"That's what I thought," she mumbled back, her eyes never leaving the long, ragged line of yellow spray paint that sprawled out before us.

It wasn't whole, not anymore. It was a faded mess, legible only if you knew what it'd said in the first place. You wouldn't know the handwriting unless you'd seen it recently, oh, say, in a note somebody slipped under a door.

"Who put Ellen in the blackgum tree," Judith read quietly.

I pulled up the camera function on my phone and held it up. "A question for the ages." The digital lens strained and focused, and most of the message filled the screen. I backed up and motioned for Judith to move over so I could get the whole thing in the shot.

She accommodated me, shifting to the right and stopping just half a step behind me. She held her phone in her hands, but she wasn't looking at it. She hadn't taken her eyes off the yellow line of text, each letter maybe a foot high. "A question for the ages, yes."

But not for us. Ours was narrower in scope. "Was she our Ellen? How do we find out for sure?"

"Dearest, if we knew that we wouldn't be roaming the town, looking at graffiti. You say 'time-wasting' and 'sight-seeing,' but I say 'brainstorming.' Or maybe 'evidence collecting.'" She finally took a picture or two, then examined them briefly on the screen.

"All we're doing is flailing around, grabbing at straws. If we were proper detectives, we could go on the hunt for the person who's been leaving these … these freaky portents, or whatever they are. They've been doing this for more than forty years."

"So, we're not proper detectives. We can still go looking for him."

"Him?"

"Masculine pronoun for the sake of laziness, but okay, you're right. It's just as likely to be a woman." She tucked her phone into her purse. "But where would we begin?"

I gazed from one end of the message to the other, then to the walls and crumbling foundations and boarded windows around it. The letters themselves crossed three plywood-covered windows and bled a dingy yellow down the bricks below them. "Here, I guess."

"And what are we learning from here? What does the yellow question tell us?"

I made a feeble effort to push back. "You're not my teacher anymore, Judith."

"No, and you're not my student. It's only an exercise. Ask me the same question, if you don't have an answer."

"All right: What does the yellow query tell you?"

She took a deep breath, and her eyes narrowed as she let it out. She interrogated every speck of paint with her eyes. "It tells me … that someone knew—or believed they knew—who the body in the tree belonged to. Shall we assume that our riddler is correct?"

"Okay."

"For the sake of argument then. A woman named Ellen was murdered and stuffed into a blackgum tree. Someone both knew her identity and declined to come forward to provide it. Did the someone in question murder her?"

"Do we know for a fact that she was murdered?" I asked, remembering how Judith traditionally felt about broad leaps and big assumptions.

"Not strictly, but the suggestion was present in the autopsy. Scraps of fabric were found in her mouth and throat. The authorities thought she'd likely been smothered to death, or maybe drowned. It was a long time ago, and her body had dried out by then. I guess they couldn't tell." Judith left me then to climb a flaking set of steps to get a closer look. I stayed where I was and let her talk her way through whatever she was thinking. "It's a damn shame the autopsy was lost and an even bigger shame that her body went AWOL. A handy-dandy DNA test could clear up everything in a matter of weeks, couldn't it?"

"It's the silver bullet in every cop show."

"But we are not so lucky. Whoever wrote this, though … did they kill her? Sometimes criminals may tease the police and return to the scene of their crimes. Like an arsonist who shows up to watch a building burn or a serial killer who sidles up to an investigation."

"I don't think so. It's just a gut feeling." I joined her at the top of the steps. There were only about six of them, each one more decrepit than the last. I tiptoed in my Toms where Judith had strolled in her Bettye Mullers.

Judith said to me, and a little to herself, "Now take a moment, evaluate the evidence, and tell me why."

I nodded as I read the oversized letters again and again. "Because … this feels more like an appeal for help. Someone unable to come forward for some reason, but still wants the world to know what happened."

She nodded too. Approvingly, I'd like to think. "The graffiti artist asks no question as to the woman's identity, and no question with regards to how she died. Does that mean our mystery artist already knows how she met her end?"

"His question here isn't how, but who. The killer would already know the answer to both."

Judith recapped in full-on teacher mode, all protests to the contrary. "Right. Very good, yes. That means we likely have a third party in play—someone who knew this Ellen, and doesn't understand what happened to her and is unable or unwilling to come forward and formally identify her."

"They probably thought they'd hinted hard enough to point the cops in the right direction," I proposed. "They fully expected a limited number of missing 'Ellens' and were either wrong about the pool of potential victims or wrong about the competence of the police."

She shrugged and turned around, heading back down the stairs. "Probably a little of Column A … and a little of Column B. Let's go. We've seen the message, and—"

"And did it actually tell us anything new?"

"Yes," she said without looking back to make sure I was following. "This was the most recent graffiti, as far as I could learn. It's at least … what? Let's say a year old, maybe older than that. Nothing new has appeared since then."

"We don't know that for certain."

"Technically, no. But let's take it as a given for now. Someone out there still cares after forty years. Or they cared as recently as a year ago. According to most of what I turned up, these messages aren't an annual event. They happen here and there, or now and then— that would be a better way to put it."

She reached the car a little before me, but I'd locked it behind us, so she had to wait while I said, "That means we're dealing with somebody at least fifty or sixty years old. Someone who was ten years old, bare minimum, when the deed occurred."

"Let's say fifteen. The handwriting has always appeared mature to me. It belonged to an adult, or someone who was nearly an adult in the seventies." Judith jiggled the car handle, and I used the button to pop the locks.

We both climbed inside.

I sat behind the wheel. I didn't put the key in the ignition right away. I still had one eye on the faded yellow message on the side of the train station. "But spray paint isn't an adult's medium when it comes to relaying important messages."

"Not typically," she agreed. She fastened her seat belt, and I started the car. "An adult might put an anonymous classified ad in the paper or staple signs to telephone poles. An adult could rent a billboard. There are a million more refined ways to ask a question, so you might be on to something there."

The tires churned into the knee-high grass and broken concrete as I turned the car around, ready to take us back out the way we'd arrived. "Where are we going next? You said there's a fire road and the tree is out there?"

She pulled out her phone and drew up the notes. "Got it, yes. Hang on, let me pull up a map."

She did, and it worked as far as the fire road. That's where Siri told us to turn around and mind our own business—or she would have if her AI had been any better.

At Judith's urging, I initially began to follow the little road, such as it was. I turned carefully onto what was really more like a dirt path and drove about five miles an hour, scarcely tapping the gas and ready to hit the brakes at any moment. It was worse than the road to the train station and worse than the ratted-out lot beside it. You could hardly even call it a road with a straight face; it was just two ruts and a grass mohawk between them. I had no idea how fire trucks were supposed to navigate it if indeed that's what a fire road was for.

I wanted to ask Judith, but I didn't want her to slide back into teacher mode, so I didn't. I just kept my eyes on the ruts and prayed that my Honda wouldn't shake itself to pieces.

After maybe a mile, I gave up. The ruts widened into a clearing and there was just room enough to turn around, so that's what I did.

Judith was displeased. "What are you doing? We're going the right way, don't stop now."

"Not like this. This car is only a lease, for Christ's sake. This is the first spot I've seen where it looked like there was room to do a 180, so I'm doing a 180 before we're trapped at some dead end. We can walk it from here."

"But it's another mile, at least!"

"Do you have any other shoes on hand?"

She looked ruefully at her low, pretty heels. "I do not. On this occasion, I was not thinking ahead. Goddammit."

"What's your shoe size?"

"About a seven, why?"

"Close enough," I told her. I turned off the car and got out, then used the key fob to pop the trunk. "I have some rain boots back here."

"But I don't have any socks!"

I tried not to be too amused by how scandalized she sounded, but it was fucking funny. "You're wearing pantyhose, and these boots are lined with fleece. You'll be fine."

She fussed and grumbled and stood beside me looking into the trunk. The rain boots were ankle-height and shiny black. "See? Look, they go with everything. Even linen slacks."

"They're a silk blend."

I rolled my eyes. "My mistake, madam. Now are you going to wear the boots or are we going to drive back empty-handed? Because I'll be honest with you, I don't care either way. I think the tree is gone, and I think the internet is wrong, and I think it's just plain crazy to go to all this trouble to find that out first-hand."

She answered me by sitting on the bumper and taking off her heels. She seized the first boot and jammed it roughly onto her foot like it'd done her wrong somehow. The second boot followed, and I shut her pretty-pretty princess shoes in the trunk for safekeeping. Then I locked the car—out of OCD more than strict necessity—and I told her to queue up the map on her phone. "I want to know exactly how far we're supposed to hike."

"Another …" She held up the phone, hunting for more than two bars. "… One-point-one miles. Allegedly."

"That's not so bad. We can do that in twenty minutes."

"Twenty minutes?"

I started walking, sticking to the middle tuft of grass where the footing was more stable. "Twenty or thirty, depending on how slow you feel like marching. The weather's nice and we've got time. Come on; if we're doing this, let's get it over with."

She fell into step beside me, falling a little behind. The grass midway wasn't wide enough for two people to walk abreast, and she was struggling with the borrowed footwear. My boots were size eight, so they were surely a little big; I heard her feet catching and flopping as she trudged. I wished I had some socks to offer her. I wished she'd thought ahead and worn something more sensible. I wished I could get her to let go of whatever morbid notion made her want to see the tree where some Ellen was left some forty-odd years ago.

But I couldn't, and I knew it; and if you can't beat 'em, join 'em.

Or lead 'em, since I was still ahead in this offbeat hike.

We hadn't gone far when I heard a familiar noise that I couldn't immediately place. We were walking through the woods on a bright, warmish day that just barely smelled like fall. The trees were still largely green and somewhat yellow and just a bit orange. I had a sweater tied around my waist and sunglasses that kept sliding down my nose.

I was distracted by it all, and I could hardly be blamed for not recalling where I'd heard the noise before—not right away.

But I did hear it. It lingered and repeated, a jagged rhythm that wasn't clean enough to dance to.

If it were dark, perhaps—if I were walking along in pajama shorts and a tank top and barefoot because my flip-flops were too wet to wear—then I might have known it in a hot second and not in a confused half a minute.

Judith stopped, and I stopped too. "What the hell is that?" she asked, scanning the surroundings.

It was coming from off to our left, not far from the trail.

I prophesied: "It's the sound of somebody digging."

"Digging what? Digging where? Digging why?"

"Who knows," I replied distractedly.

Something in the trees moved. Something in a long gray dress, with a shock of long, black hair that curled and coiled. But it wasn't dark outside, and this wasn't the hotel, so I hadn't seen it. I hadn't seen her, with a finger to her lips and a gleam in her eyes. I hadn't seen anything. I would've sworn it if anybody had asked.

"What was that? Over there."

"No," I said, without even looking to see which way she was pointing. "There's nothing and nobody out here."

"I did see something. A second ago, I could've sworn. Look," she said with determination. Then with confusion, "Well, I guess she's gone now."

The sound was gone too. Or rather, it had stopped.

"What are you doin' here?"

We both snapped to attention and then to our left where a woman stood just inside the tree line. She was tall and broad, somewhere between my age and Judith's. Her hair was graying and her work boots were covered in mud. She leaned on the handle of a shovel.

"Hello?" I said stupidly.

"I asked you a question."

Judith cleared her throat and assumed her best air of scholarly authority combined with genteel southern ladylikeness. "That you did, and I must apologize for both of us. Are we ... are we trespassing? I know this used to be private land—"

"It's still private land."

"Not yours though. Is it?" she asked, ending the question on a slightly higher pitch. "For that matter, what are you doing out here? Are you all right? Do you need help?" Oh, Judith. One of the greatest lessons she ever taught me was how to ingratiate with offers of assistance. I've never seen it not work.

The woman furrowed her brow and adjusted her hold on the shovel. "No, this isn't my land. Shit, I don't know who owns it anymore," she confessed. "And no, I don't need any help. I'm all finished for now."

"Good, I'm glad to know that. However, my friend and I ... we could use some assistance. We're looking for a certain tree—" she began.

The woman snorted. "'Course you are. 'Course you are," she said again, under her breath. "The blackgum tree? That's what you're out here for? More goddamn atrocity tourists."

"No," I jumped in before she could melt back into the woods with the ghosts. "No, we're not tourists, exactly. We're more like ... investigators."

"Investigators?"

I removed my sunglasses. "My aunt, she disappeared back in the late seventies, and—"

"And her name was Ellen. Got it."

"Yes, her name was Ellen. She was the right age, the right general description, and she lived in Nashville. So ... not that far from here. We think she might've come here, doing research for a doctoral thesis." Okay, so that part was a stretch—but it was an opening.

"I wouldn't know anythin' about that."

Judith stumbled forward, tripping over the boots and catching herself. "It was a very long time ago, I know. You would've been a child when she passed through—if she passed through. Please, we're only looking for the truth."

"And we're trying to give my family some closure." I leaned on the family angle, as Judith had once suggested. "I know lots of other people have come looking over the years and left empty-handed. Maybe we will too. But we have to try, you know? For the sake of my grandmother." To whom I was not presently speaking, but whatever. It worked. The woman softened.

She sighed. "What good would it do you to see the tree? What do you care? The body's long gone and long lost," she told us. "Everything is."

Judith noted, "The tree's not."

She gave up. "Fine. If it's that important to you. Go another ... oh, it's not even a quarter mile, I'd say. It's on the right up ahead. There's a little clearing around it, and kids like to hang ribbons and scraps of cotton in the trees nearby. You can't miss it." Then, before we could thank her or ask her anything else, she melted back into the trees.

In another five seconds, it was like she'd never been there at all.

Judith and I stood in the grassy median between the two dirt ruts that were just too damn much for my car, staring at the spot between the trees where the woman had stood. We couldn't hear any footsteps. We couldn't see her back, retreating deeper into the woods, the shovel slung over her shoulder, bouncing with every step.

We looked at each other and tried to ask a normal question, the kind that didn't sound like two women who'd seen a ghost and didn't quite know how to discuss it.

Judith went first. "I guess my intel was ... just about right. A quarter mile ahead, she said?"

"In a clearing."

"Convenient," she said lightly. She checked her phone and pointed the way forward. "And I liked the bit about ribbons and such. They do that for clootie wells, you know. Come on then," she ordered, stepping into the lead, wearing my boots that were just enough too big that she moved a little like a duck when she walked.

"Yeah, I know. Yeah, I'm coming."

We found the tree about five minutes later. You could see the clearing from the path: a spot where the trunks thinned out in a radius of maybe ten yards around a ragged blackgum tree that had to be a hundred years old if it was a day. The gnarled old thing had holes where branches had fallen and made way for owls and woodland critters; its top limbs were drying to a brittle gray. The surviving foliage was brilliant though, almost fully turned for fall, vivid red and purple.

Around it ... nothing.

Not even grass.

"This has to be it," Judith almost whispered. "My God, look at it. It's as if it's poisoned everything around it. Nothing wants to come in close. Not even the weeds."

"Getting a tad romantic in your old age, aren't you?"

She knew I was teasing. "Better late than never."

I laughed and said, "True. This tree, though. It's kind of raggedy looking."

"Well, it's old." She took another step toward it, and I did too. "Blackgums fall apart from the top down as they get older. They get shorter."

"Like people."

"Yes, like people. If you must."

Raggedy or not, I couldn't take my eyes off it. It was like some holy thing, set apart from the world for the world's own good. Some weird oracle, some harbinger of ancient knowledge. Even the air around it was empty. No birds, no bugs. It was warm enough that there should've been mosquitos since we hadn't gotten a good freeze yet. But nothing buzzed, hummed, chirped, or sang in the tree's immediate vicinity.

Under our feet, the ground was dry clay, cracked and dull. It had split where the old tree's roots went sprawling too close to the surface, and knobby knees of winding wood jutted up through the grass like hints of earthy tentacles.

"Judith, this is messed up."

"No. It's only a tree, dear." But she wasn't smiling anymore. Neither one of us was teasing, even though that it'd always been our default interaction when we were stressed or confused.

Frankly, I was both stressed and confused; and as my companion had so bluntly pointed out, it was only a tree. Maybe there was a smell to it—something just barely detectable, a hint of rot or decaying mulch. Maybe the old thing was dying. Maybe it was killing.

"It's only a tree," I echoed her. But then I had to wonder, "But is it the tree? The one that used to hold an Ellen?"

"You know it is as well as I do."

Judith approached it, still struggling with the terrain and my boots, but calm and certain all the same. She moved like a priestess with an offering. I don't know why that comparison came to mind. I didn't like it and pushed it from my mind.

"Be careful," I warned her.

"Of what?"

I stayed where I was. "I dunno. Snakes and shit."

"You're being ridiculous." She was underneath it now, the brilliant canopy bathing her in the muted light of colored shadows. "Forty years ago, give or take," her hand stretched out, her fingers grazing the trunk, "someone stuffed a woman's body right here. Right in this fork, I expect. What a preposterous thing to do. Why not bury her? Why not … dissolve her in a bathtub full of acid, or chop her up and burn her to ashes?"

"Jesus, Judith."

"I'm being serious. If you didn't want the body found, why wouldn't you take steps to hide it? Or dispose of it more formally, more thoroughly than this … this act of display, if that's what it was."

I was getting warm standing in the sun, but I'd sooner melt than get any closer to that tree. It wasn't the raggedy appearance, and it wasn't the smattering of rags and ribbons that had been tied around it. Something was wrong there, that's all I can say. It had all the trappings of a clootie well, but no water to be seen. Unless that's what the woman with the shovel had been digging. "No one found her body for a while, so it must've been a better hiding place than you'd think. Look around. We're in the middle of nowhere. It's a miracle she was ever found at all."

She shook her head. "Not a miracle. An accident. Two different things."

"Either way, it's weird."

"A tidy summing up of the matter, yes." She was still staring up at the fork, presumably higher now than it'd been in 1978 or 1979. I expect she was thinking the same thing and pondering how difficult it might've been to jam a corpse all the way up there. If you could do it alone, or if you needed a friend.

I was thinking about all the sun-faded scraps of cotton that were tied on the lowest limbs and dangled from the closest vegetation. When I glanced at the ground, I saw that I was standing on one such scrap, folded and bleached beneath my foot.

I took out my cell phone and snapped a few pics, mostly to justify the fact that I was keeping my distance. I couldn't stand the thought of coming even one foot closer to that beautiful, cursed thing in the clearing. It was nonsense and I knew it, but I couldn't fight it. It was madness, and I knew that too. It was only a tree, standing alone in the woods, a little way off a fire road in the geographic center of Godforsaken, Bumblefuck, USA.

Judith remained enthralled, stroking the tree as if she could reach through time and touch whatever used to be there. She stopped and sat down so she could rest against the trunk. She sighed, not quite happily, but almost.

"You actually believe it was her," I said flatly.

"I suspect it was, yes. I'm tempted to say that I hope it was, but of course, I don't. Or I do, but only in a complicated and selfish way. I hope that Ellen was not murdered and lost to the world, but somehow, I also hope to have an answer—one day. Even if it's this one. Does that make me a terrible person?"

Still, I stayed put. One of us needed to be free of this weird spell, or whatever it was. "No, I get it. Even if the truth is terrible, you'd like to hear it eventually. Especially since there's nothing you can do about it now. Might as well know for certain."

"We won't find certainty here."

"You know what I meant."

"I always do," she said. She closed her eyes and leaned her head back against the bark. "And here's the thing, honey: I've been telling myself for all these years that if I ever found the truth, I'd know it. With or without any proper evidence to support it."

"And you're feeling it now—that certainty?"

"Yes, I'm feeling it now."

I wasn't feeling anything in particular, except a powerful sense that I'd rather be almost anywhere else in the world. I put my phone away and shifted my weight from foot to foot. "Can we go?"

She acted like she hadn't heard me. "It's almost comforting, sitting here. Knowing—or feeling and believing—that she was here too. Nothing separates us but time."

"Nothing separates you from a corpse, Judith. A corpse that might have been Ellen's."

"There are worse places to be dead. She was here for nearly two years, that's what the coroner thought at the time. Two years, two sets of seasons. Seven hundred and thirty days of sun and rain. Winter and warmth. Perched in the branches, like some kind of offering."

"Wedged in the trunk, like discarded trash. Don't mythologize this, Judith. It won't do anyone any good. Not even you."

She opened her eyes to scowl at me, but I didn't care. If getting out of there took pissing her off, I was down for it. "What's gotten into you?" she asked.

"Gravel in my shoes and a powerful, growing thirst. I need water. I need shelter. I need to go back to the car, and this is crazy. Come on, please? You've seen the tree. It's very tree-like, and I'm sorry to ruin this moment for you, but I'm leaving. If you want some time alone, that's fine. I'll be in the car."

I turned and left, but I left slowly, giving her time to collect herself and follow.

"You don't have to be like that," she chided as she caught up.

"Apparently, I do if I want your attention. This is creepy and not in a good way. Don't fetishize that tree. I can't stand it. It's awful, and don't ask me why." I stomped through the grass, back toward the road.

She drew up alongside me. "I wasn't going to."

"You were thinking about it. Now come on. When we get back to the car, we can queue the address you found. I'm not in a great rush to badger some woman about something traumatic that happened when she was a kid, but anything's better than staying out here, hanging out with the murder tree."

"To think, you had the nerve to suggest I was mythologizing the thing."

"Oh, hush."

CHAPTER SEVEN

JUDITH and I drove back to town and stopped for lunch at the same little diner as before. Our options were few, and anyway, I think we were stalling our trip to see one of the women who discovered the corpse when she was a child. We split a large pepperoni pizza and made small talk until I pressed for details.

"Seriously, Judith—what are we going to say to this woman?"

"The same thing a hundred other people have said already, I expect." She pushed a sliver of crust into a small pile of parmesan cheese and smushed it until it collected most of the pale, delicious dust. "It's obvious, isn't it? Dozens of people have undoubtedly looked her up over the years, wanting interviews for puff pieces, tidbits of additional information as the search for lost loved ones, hell, more than a few probably came out from universities."

"What for?"

"Research." She bit off the tasty end of the crust, chewed, and swallowed. "Off the top of my head, I can think of several great projects. The case of Ellen in the blackgum tree could be tackled from any number of angles—how dead women are treated in the press, the handling of evidence in the course of small-town politics, how urban legends are formed and spread—the possibilities are just about endless."

"Cinderwich is hardly urban, and this particular Ellen was no legend. She was real."

She flipped her hand dismissively. "Call it a rural legend, then, if you must be a stickler for vocabulary. Facts are thin on the ground, Kate. There's no evidence at all, short of oral history and a few articles lost in the archives of a little old library branch. You went there already, yes?"

"I told you I did. The librarian said the tree was gone."

Judith nodded. "That's right. You see what I mean? In the absence of concrete evidence, all oral history must remain suspect. The librarian was wrong about the tree and she could be wrong about anything else."

"So could anybody who heard anything passed down through the grapevine. Or any witness testimony, like you hope to gain from this woman we're about to intrude on. It's notoriously unreliable."

"Well, isn't everything?"

I felt like she was talking in circles, and that wasn't like her. Not usually. I wondered if it was because she felt so close—within arm's reach of the answers she'd clawed toward for decades. Was the gravitational force warping her perspective? Was she just getting old?

"Pardon me for a minute," she declared. She slipped out of the booth and dragged her purse in her wake. "I need to powder my nose."

I grinned. I don't think she's ever used the word "toilet" in her life. "I hope everything comes out all right."

"Knock it off." She returned the smile anyway and headed for the back of the restaurant.

I was finished eating, so I did what I always do when I'm left to my own devices and pulled out my phone. I checked my email, glanced at Twitter, and then I remembered I'd taken a few shots of the creepy tree beside the fire road. It'd been too bright outside to get a really good look at them, and I'd been rattled enough that I hadn't tried too hard. I'd only wanted to leave.

I checked them now out of idle curiosity.

The first one was a vaguely tree-shaped smudge; apparently, I'd been a tad too wiggly when I snapped it. But the two or three before that one were pretty sharp.

There they were: perfectly clear images of a large, aging tree with vivid foliage and a dying top canopy. A split in its trunk led to two main branches, and a thin white woman was standing before it—then sitting against it. "Judith, you really are crazy sometimes," I told the screen. She wouldn't have argued if I'd said it to her face. She would have only said something like, "Even a broken clock's right twice a day." Then I would say back, "You mean, the sun shines on a dog's ass every once in a while." Then she would roll her eyes, and I'd laugh.

The old patterns were so easy, so familiar. I could almost fanfic them—even predict them, as if they were alternate timelines depicting how our conversations might go.

I swiped through the pictures, squinting at the small screen. They were exactly what I'd seen when I'd stood there at a distance. They were exactly what they should've been, except for how they weren't. I went back to the first shot I'd taken, the one where the tree was a vaguely arboreal smear. There was a second smear, a very small one behind it and to the right. A sliver of smoke.

I swiped. The next picture was clearer.

No, not a streak or a sliver, but a long gray dress. A dark mass above it, nothing below. The next picture. The mass was a long, winding cloud of hair with a snow-white face that had no eyes.

Next picture.

Had I taken this many? I didn't remember taking this many. Had the phone been on burst mode? It must have been. It was the only thing that made sense.

Next picture. Now she had eyes again, large and round and doll-like. Too bright for a real face. Too human for a phantom. One more swipe. There she was again, closer to Judith. Not sneaking up, so much as merely being closer this time. And the next time, in the next picture.

No, she hadn't been there. No, I hadn't seen her. No, there had been a woman in gray, tiptoeing between the trees on tiny bare feet that never quite touched the ground.

But there she was anyway in picture after picture.

In the last one, she was so close that Judith could've reached out and tickled her toes. But Judith only sat there against the tree, leaning her head back, throat exposed, with her eyes closed and the oddest smile on her face. The woman in gray wasn't looking at her. She was looking at me, and she held one finger up to her lips.

The bathroom door swung open, and I slammed the phone down like it'd bitten me.

"You all right?" Judith asked as she slid back into the booth.

"Fine. Why? And don't tell me that I look like I've seen a ghost. I hate that expression. It's stupid."

She frowned at me and pushed her plate away. She dropped a wadded-up napkin on it. "I wasn't going to, but all right, now I definitely won't. What's got you so rattled?"

"I'm not rattled."

"You're clearly rattled."

"Leave it alone," I told her. I turned off my phone and stuck it back in my purse. "Just an annoying text message, nothing to do with this. Or you. Or Ellen," I lied through my teeth. "Are you ready to go? I'm ready to go."

She let me hang there for a few seconds, deciding whether or not to believe me. Or whether or not to challenge me, perhaps. (Yes, that was more likely.) I was relieved when in the end, she said, "Fine. I've got the address to her house right here. Put it in your phone and let's get this over with."

"If you don't want to do this—"

"You know that I do. Come on, here it is." She pushed a slip of paper across the table, and I took it.

I retrieved my phone and plugged the street address into the map. "3223 Riverhead Street In Cinderwich, I assume?"

"Outside it a bit."

"Yeah, but for robot phone lady purposes," I muttered, as Siri tried to send me to a version of that address in the middle of Ohio. I clarified "Cinderwich" in the app and the system struggled but then pulled it up. "She's about a mile from here. We could practically walk."

"Not on your life," Judith said firmly. "I've already got blisters from those ridiculous rubber boots of yours."

"You can't possibly." I grabbed my purse and pulled out a few bucks for a tip. I left it on the table. "Come on, you. Let's go harass an old lady about the most traumatic day of her life."

She reminded me, "She won't be old. She was maybe eight when the body was found. She's barely any older than you. I'd be thrilled to see such a tender age again."

"I'm well on my way, so go ahead and tell me how great it was."

"Sorry, I'm too old. Can't remember."

I turned around and gave her a little nudge with my elbow, then held the door for her. It shut behind us with the jangle of a string of bells tied together with what looked like a boot lace.

Then we got back into my car, and I put my phone in the holder that keeps it jammed upright in one of the AC vents. "Okay, Siri. How do we get to this woman's house …" I mumbled as I pressed the green "go" button on the screen.

Five minutes later, we pulled up in front of 3223 Riverhead Street, and it was everything I could've asked for.

Three stories tall, Victorian, and well-kept if somewhat worn around the edges, the house was a majesty of gothic architecture— the home Gomez and Morticia would've built if they'd ever cared to live in rural Tennessee. It had once been dark gray, and in some spots it still was. In others, it had faded to the shade of a dress a ghost might wear.

No. I was being ridiculous.

It was only an old house, with gingerbread and columns, and a widow's walk squaring off the top of one tower. The other was rounded with a circular window of decorative glass. Nothing was broken, exactly, and nothing was dirty. It was merely old and beautiful and clearly loved, and if you'd moved it closer to the city, I might've died on the spot just so I could haunt it later on.

We sat together in the car, staring at this marvelous place. There wasn't a driveway to speak of, so we were just parked at the edge of the road, pulled onto the shoulder. Or rather, we were half in the ditch because there wasn't a shoulder either.

Judith pulled down the visor to check her makeup in the mirror. She clutched her purse with one hand and took the door latch with the other. "Here goes nothing," she said with determination. Then, before I could protest any further, she'd opened the door and was standing wobblily beside the car.

The ditch's grade was steeper than it looked. I hadn't meant to park so close or make her lean so hard or balance so precariously in her heels. I got out too. I quickly went around to the passenger side and offered her my hand. "Come on, get out of that. Over here." I guided her toward the brick walkway that led to the front door.

"I don't need any help."

"I do. This place is creepy as shit," I lied again. I was never very good at it, not when Judith was involved. I'm sure she saw right through me, but she was lying too when she said she didn't require assistance.

She leaned on me until all four of our feet had found the walkway. "You're right about that. This place is quite a … production."

"A production?"

"I can't think of a better word that doesn't sound unkind." She gently shook my hand loose and straightened herself. "Now. Let's go say hello."

I tagged along half a step behind her, reluctantly walking up to this gorgeous house that Judith hated. I wanted to see inside it out of pure nosiness, but I didn't want to interrogate anybody for the opportunity to do so. I let her take the lead because I didn't want it and wouldn't know what to do with it if I had it.

Up a short flight of porch stairs we climbed, and we stood together in front of an oversized front door with three round windows across the top. I'd never seen anything quite like it, but the hardware and glass all looked original. I admired it while Judith took hold of a large iron knocker.

"I would've called first," she told me quietly. "But as far as I can tell, the ladies don't have a phone. Or maybe they have cells and that's why they're not in the phone book."

The librarian had called them that too: the ladies. It didn't exactly mean anything, but it stuck in my head regardless.

Judith knocked.

We waited. We listened and heard the faintest of footsteps descending stairs, crossing a foyer, and pausing on the other side of the door. An eye appeared in the centermost piece of circular glass. The eye narrowed.

"Who's there?"

Judith cleared her throat. "Hello, and I beg your pardon. My name is Judith Kane, and this is my friend, Kate Thrush. I was wondering if we could chat with you for just a few minutes. If you could be so kind."

I did my best to look innocuous and helpful and probably succeeded at neither.

There was a pause. Then the turn of a lock and the twist of a knob. The door swung inward.

The woman inside did not speak right away. She just looked us up and down, one at a time, through a pair of small wire-framed glasses. The lenses were shaped like diamonds, giving her an air that was one part wholly skeptical and one part elfin. Her hair was mostly black and partly a deep shade of pink, and it hung nearly to her waist. She was dressed in shades of black and gray from head to toe, accented with lace and covered with a gauzy light sweater that ended in a fringe around her knees. Her fingers were weighed down with bright silver rings, many of which had sparkling eyes. At a glance, I saw a crow, a dragon, and a lion.

She was in every way perfect—the platonic ideal of what I imagined the owner of such a house must be. It was all I could do not to blurt, "Oh my God!" I only stopped myself with the thought that it might not amuse her and might in fact offend her.

I put my hand to my mouth.

The woman raised an eyebrow; it peaked neatly, pointing away from some glittery red eyeshadow and a pair of maroon-painted lips. She said, "Journalists."

I said, "What?" and Judith said, "No."

"Ghost show TV hosts."

I said, "Jesus," and Judith said, "Hardly."

Her third guess was the charm. "You think you know who Ellen was."

I nodded. "There you go. That's the one."

Judith held out her hand. "Are you Ms. Jillienne Venterman? I'm Dr. Judith Kane, and this is Kate Thrush. We think Cinderwich's Ellen was Kate's aunt, and my dearest friend, Ellen Thrush."

She shook Judith's hand. "Sure, why not."

"I'm sorry?" I asked.

She smiled. "I only meant, yes—I'm the woman you're looking for, and yes, she was as likely your Ellen as anyone else's. Here, you might as well come inside. Let me get you some tea. Do you do tea?" Before we could answer, she'd turned away and was gesturing for us to follow, her fingers glittering as she went. "Of course, you do tea. Everyone does tea."

I did as instructed, struggling to conceal my glee.

Much like its hostess, the house was a perfect and complete example of exactly what it should've been: charmingly dark, though there were plenty of windows. Everything black, with purple or red accents and gleams of silver. I saw little altars, here and there, and esoteric artwork that featured women and ghosts and water.

She chattered on as she led us deeper into the house. "You're actually the first people to come by in quite a while. I know there's a new article about our mysterious Ellen making the rounds—something from the Chattanooga paper, isn't it? Usually, that means a fresh round of curiosity seekers, but they've become fewer and farther between in the last ... oh, ten years, I'd say." She paused and turned to look at us. She chose eye contact with Judith, not me, when she said, "Perhaps you'll be the last, and we'll all get the answers we've been looking for."

Then she proceeded to lure us into the rear of the enormous home, where the kitchen was. We passed a grand formal dining room right next to it, but she ushered us to a smaller eat-in arrangement in front of a big bay window and urged us to sit.

She glanced at the clock. "Hmm, my sister ought to be home in a bit. I'll do a big pot and she can join us if she likes."

I took a seat at a black round table, its shiny top protected by black lace place mats. Judith pulled out a chair too. "Your sister lives here with you?" she asked, even though I knew good and well that she knew it already.

"Two sisters do, after a fashion. One of blood and one of the heart. We have each other, and it's quite enough to keep us happy." Jillienne turned a dial on a vintage gas stove, prompting the click click click to start the flames. She filled the pot and set it down to boil.

"That must be nice," I said, keeping up the small talk. "A house this size could get lonely if you were all by yourself."

"It might," she agreed, collecting several teacups from a glass cabinet. "Then again, it might not. With or without my sisters, I'd always have the ghosts."

"The house is haunted?"

She nodded and added a couple of saucers to her haul before setting it in front of us. "Only a little. Cold spots, shadows, and the like. They're hardly ghosts anymore. They're more like memories—

bits and pieces of people who the house hasn't forgotten yet." Returning to the cabinet, she collected a spinning display case stocked with a dozen or more varieties of loose tea and little metal strainers. She presented it to us and urged us to select whatever we wanted.

I picked a blackberry cassis. I'm not sure what Judith chose.

"And I'll take … oh, the Earl Grey for Camille." The pot itself was a pink and white confection with gold trim to match the cups and saucers. She lingered beside it as it warmed on the stove. "So! There's rather a lot you need to know when it comes to the woman who might've been your Ellen. I'm not entirely sure where to begin. Do you have any specific questions?"

I was caught off guard, but Judith wasn't. Judith was always ready with questions. "I suppose I should start with the simplest of basics: You are one of the girls who found the body, yes?"

"Yes," she nodded. "I was the oldest of us." She laughed to herself and picked a hand towel off the counter. "I'm still the oldest of us, of course. That's how time usually works. But yes, I was nine years old. My sister Camille was seven, and so was our friend, Liana."

"What about the other two girls?" I wanted to know. "There were five of you. Isn't that right?"

Ms. Venterman darkened. She nodded again, more slowly this time. "Elise and Marie. They were cousins who lived in the city with their grandparents. They drowned a few years later—you must know that, or you wouldn't have asked."

The city? She probably meant Chattanooga. It was the closest bit of civilization that might qualify. "Did they … drown at the same time?" I followed up weakly. Judith had told me, but I couldn't remember.

"No, they died …" she thought about it, "… maybe a few years apart. One drowned in a well on her mother's farm, and the other drowned in the river."

"Quite a coincidence," Judith observed.

"Hardly. But therein lies another story—a story that's only adjacent to the one you'd like to hear." The kettle started to rattle but didn't boil. She gave it a little stink-eye, and it stopped shaking.

"The story you want to hear—that's either quick and easy or long and tough, depending on which version strikes your fancy."

"Let's start easy," she suggested.

"All right." Jillienne paused as the kettle spit out a thin curl of steam and the water inside began to hum. She leaned back against the counter next to the stove and loosely folded her arms. "It was a Thursday morning in the middle of summer. We were turned loose, sent outside, and told to entertain ourselves until dark—like parents used to do back then. We'd all meet up at the edge of our neighborhood where the state road crossed through and the stop sign had half a dozen bullet holes in it."

I did a little laugh. "That sounds ... safe."

She waved away any worries. "Oh, it was fine. It was just our friend Cheryl's brother, who got drunk one night and thought he was shooting at the moon. Or something, I'm not sure, but that's how I heard it."

"I had a cousin like that," I admitted. "My uncle took his gun away after someone called the cops. He'd been trying to scare a raccoon off the top of his garage and took out a transformer on a power pole."

The teakettle's curl of steam exploded into a billowing cloud.

"Then you know from whence I speak." She took a trivet and removed the kettle, then began filling our cups. When she was finished, she took her tea and sat down with us. She wrapped her fingers around the porcelain cup, her rings clinking against it like wind chimes. "At any rate, we met at the edge of the neighborhood like we often did and negotiated the day's plans. We had heard about the fire road, but we didn't know what a fire road was. And we were very interested in finding out."

"Did you think it was a road made of fire?" Judith asked.

"Made of fire, leading to fire—we had no idea. Mind you, Marie's mother had strictly forbidden us from going anywhere near it, but Marie and Elise were never the strictly obedient type, and the rest of us weren't either."

I sipped, but the tea was still hot and so was the cup. I set it back down in its saucer. "Why didn't the adults want you exploring it?"

"I think they were afraid we'd follow it too long and wander too far. If we got tired after following a road for a couple of miles, we'd have to walk back—or someone would have to come find us. In retrospect, it was a reasonable enough thing to forbid, but we didn't listen, and we decided to see for ourselves what a fire road was."

She offered us cream and sugar. Judith and I helped ourselves.

"We were children, please remember. Don't judge us too harshly." She fixed her tea with a spoonful of sugar and stirred it. "But we met that morning, and we were prepared, let me tell you. We'd packed sandwiches and Little Debbies, and we'd brought a flashlight. Liana had a pocketknife, and I had a box of matches. Camille had a thermos full of water. We really thought it through." She laughed gently to herself. She sobered with a sigh and continued. "We reached the road in half an hour, and we were disappointed—it was only a road, no fire to be seen. It wasn't even paved, not really. Just a couple of ruts with a grass median between them."

"We saw it," I told her. "Earlier today, we went to take a look. It still looks exactly like that."

"Not much to it, is there?"

"No," Judith agreed with her. "Nothing to write home about."

"Ah, but for all we knew, there was fire at the end of it. That was the conclusion we reached—five silly girls who'd heard two words put together and needed to make sense of them. We started hiking, and we kept going until the sun got high and we got warm. We decided to take a little break and eat those Little Debbies before they got too melted and mushed. Marie, oh—she'd brought a Coke too, come to think of it. We all shared everything, back then.

"So anyway, we stopped. There was this tree …" She raised one hand off the cup and waved it, indicating something large and fluffy. "It was set apart from the other trees, just off the side of the road. It had these big, knotty roots sticking up; they were perfect for sitting on, and the trunk was perfect for leaning against. There were ribbons everywhere, I remember that. Each one a little wish, waving in the breeze …" Her voice wandered away and then came back. "It was shady and cool, and a good place to regroup. By then, we'd started to argue."

Judith toyed with her tea, turning the cup around by its handle. "About what?"

"Oh, you know. It was hot and we were getting bored. We knew we'd have to walk back eventually. The question was the quest: If we kept going, would we find any fire? How much longer should we go before we give up? When should we conclude that the trip was a bust and head home?

"But then I … I heard something." She struggled with her words and picked a few quite carefully. "That's as closely as I can explain it. I heard a voice, but I couldn't hear what it was saying. It was a whisper from someplace far away. I thought it came from above, but I couldn't be sure."

We all took a sip of our tea like we'd all been prompted by the same unease. It had cooled enough to be perfect in our mouths, a tiny bit sharp and sour and a tiny bit sweet.

"But I heard it, and I looked up. The first thing I saw was a shoe. It was dark, but so dirty I couldn't tell you what color it'd been the last time anyone had worn it. The shoe was a pump, with a short heel that was just thick enough to call chunky. I told Camille because she was closest. I said, 'Do you see that shoe? Isn't that funny?' She agreed that it was funny, and we had a laugh about it.

"But it wasn't an easy laugh. Even before we'd seen the rest, we all felt like something was off. It might've been the heat, or we might've all been tired and hungry. But there was something in the air, and it whispered … I still heard those whispers. They were saying to look harder, that's what I think."

"But you can't be sure?" Judith asked.

"No, I can't be sure. I never could. We all heard her though."

"Her?"

"The whisperer. We all heard her, and we all looked again. It was Camille who said it first—she said, 'That looks like a stocking. It looks like a leg.' It didn't really look like a leg, not anymore. It looked like someone had put a tree limb down inside a pair of nylons. Most of the flesh was gone, and what was left was all the wrong color." She stopped herself suddenly. Her rings clicked hard against the cup. "Oh, I'm sorry! I don't mean to be insensitive if this is your Ellen. I apologize, I really do. You don't need or want those details—not if she was yours."

"It's fine." Judith said it with a smile, but her face was a little tight. If you didn't know her, you probably wouldn't have noticed it. "Tell the story however you need to. It's been a very long time."

"Go on," I also urged. "I never met the woman, and if Judith says she's okay, she's okay."

Jillienne shrugged. "As you like, but I have to tell you—it wasn't pretty. She was barely a corpse. By that point, you'd almost have to call what was left of her 'remains.' She hung there, not exactly wedged in place. She'd been there long enough that the tree'd begun to grow around her. I guess you could say she was trapped there, tangled in the bark and branches. Her head was leaning down and to the right. It rested on a limb there, face-down. I couldn't see her face," she emphasized quickly. "Just the back and side of her head and her hair. It was curly and a washed-out shade of light brown."

We were all quiet for a few seconds, until Judith said, "You girls must've screamed your heads off."

"Oh no," she protested. "We didn't do that. We didn't know what we were looking at. Was it a mannequin? A doll? A puppet? For all we could tell, she might not be any bigger than any of us. We were sitting on the ground, you remember. We were so small, ourselves. We each figured out the truth on our own. It took us a minute, and we stared, and we tried to think of anything it could be, except for what it was.

"At first, we didn't talk about it. At first, we put our food and drinks away and went to stand at the edge of the clearing, where we could see the road that would take us home. We stood in the sun, sweating and stalling, not knowing what to do. I pulled an old blue ribbon off a bush and made a wish; I didn't know what else to do. We couldn't just leave her there, but we couldn't tell anyone— Maria's mother was friends with our mothers, and we'd all be dead if anybody found out, we were sure of it.

"Initially, that's what we decided: we would keep it to ourselves and not say a word. We pinky-swore it, and then we spit on our palms and all shook hands. We would've done the blood-swearing thing too, except Elise was scared to death of blood and she wouldn't let Liana cut her finger. I can hardly blame her, but maybe it would've mattered. I don't know.

"We swore on it, that's the point. Then we walked home in absolute silence. It was late afternoon by the time we made it back to the shot-up stop sign. We stopped underneath it, once again swore everyone to silence, and went our separate ways. I think, even then, we all knew that someone was going to talk. I think we each considered doing so ourselves, wondering how we might spill the beans without drawing any attention to the fact that we'd been someplace where we shouldn't have gone. But when you're a small child—just a little girl, even—how do you report something anonymously?

"We couldn't just phone in a tip to the local cops. Any officer who answered the phone would've figured out who'd done it in an afternoon—we were kids, but we knew that much. Back then, you didn't have to go to Chattanooga or the state patrol if you needed the law because Cinderwich had its own station. I believe we had two whole full-time officers? That sounds right. One of them was Liana's uncle. The other was a cousin of his.

"In the end, we kept the secret longer than you might expect of five little girls. It was almost two weeks before Camille cracked."

I had been staring down into my cup, but now I perked up. "Your own sister? Et tu, Camille?"

"Right? Well, she was the youngest of us all by a few months. Really, if she hadn't let it out when she did, I might've done it for her. Those two weeks were hard for her—hard in ways I didn't understand at the time, and I do feel guilty about it now.

"She stopped sleeping through the night. She quit eating more than a mouthful at a time. She walked around with this look on her face …" Her voice faded. She drank more tea. She was buying herself time, I think. I believe she might've surprised herself, still needing a beat after all these years.

"Eventually, one morning over breakfast, she was staring down at her plate, and our mother asked what she was doing. Why wouldn't she eat. What was wrong. She looked up and said, 'I was wondering what the lady in the tree ate when she had breakfast for the last time.'"

We all went for another swig of tea, even though our cups were more than half empty by then. I was trying to think of something kind to say or intelligent to ask when Jillienne continued.

With a hint of cheer that was only barely forced, she said, "After that, the cat was out of the bag. By lunchtime, we were all five sitting in the police station with Liana's uncle shaking his head and frowning at us. Oh, we were in so much trouble. Oh, there would be a reckoning, they warned us. But first, we had to take them to the lady in the tree. The younger girls weren't likely to remember the exact location of the tree, I didn't think, so I volunteered. Do you want the truth?" she asked.

We nodded.

"I wanted to see the body again. I wanted another look. Does that sound morbid? Well then, it's morbid, I don't care. I'd been thinking of her ... God. I'd been thinking of almost nothing else ever since I first set eyes on that shoe.

"I took the police down the fire road, in the cop car this time. I remember how rough the ride was and how the tires almost got stuck in the grass. I remember concentrating to recall how far we'd gone before we'd stopped at the tree. Riding was different from walking and it threw me off. We stopped twice at the wrong spot before I finally found the right place when I saw the clootie ribbons on the bushes, on the road, on the branches: the big blackgum tree, with a huge green canopy and knobby roots that were sitting too shallow under the dirt.

"That's the second and last time I ever saw her. One of the last times anyone saw her, come to think of it. You know they lost her body, don't you?"

Judith knew it all too well. "The last record I found said that she'd been sent to Chattanooga, to the medical examiner's office there. The office made a note to send her on to Nashville where the facilities were larger and better equipped, but the office in Nashville denies ever having received her."

Jillienne nodded, impressed. "I didn't know that part. You really did your homework."

"She always does," I said, more drily than was strictly necessary.

Judith ignored my tone, or she might not have noticed it. "I hoped that maybe, somehow, she'd been shipped back here and interred in a potter's field, or whatever the local equivalent might be."

"I have no idea if we've got any such thing. There's only the one cemetery, as far as I know. Except," she gestured with her now-empty cup out the window. "for a few family plots and the like. I know a handful of those, but none of them have any unidentified graves. Usually, there aren't more than three or four stones, and everyone knows who they belong to."

I leaned forward. "But there is a cemetery. Does that mean there's a possibility? That she might've wound up there? Or here?"

"Anything's possible, but I never heard any rumor about it—and believe me, I've heard every rumor about the Cinderwich Ellen. Or I assume I have, though there's always the chance I'm wrong. You're welcome to ask my sisters when they come home. I'd be surprised if they had anything new to add, but it's been so long ... they might remember a detail or two that escapes me."

Judith said, "Between the three of you, we might get a full picture of events. Is that what you're saying?"

Jillienne smiled. "A largely redundant one, but perhaps a version with a few extra details. Give it a try, I say. Shake the family tree and see what falls out." She gazed down into the teacup and lightly swirled the dredges that remained. "Would you look at that," she murmured.

"Look at what?" I checked my own cup and saw only a few drops of tea and specks of leaves stuck to the sides.

"The leaves, if you believe in that sort of thing."

"You read them?"

"For fun. Sometimes it's only peculiar." She turned her cup to face us, but it all looked like leftover tea nonsense to me. "Here's a bit about visitors. I suppose that's you two. Here," she waved to Judith. "Let me see your cup."

She passed it over. "By all means."

Jillienne Venterman took it in her hand and swished it in a circle three times, letting the liquid settle while leaving debris along the sides. She peered inside, adjusting her grip and holding the cup by the delicate handle. "Ah, yes. A recent trip—the one you took that brought you here, I assume."

"Probably."

"And ... it's hard to say. This part looks a bit like a sun with some stars. Good omens overall. This part over here might be an owl, but let's say it isn't. Let's say that it's cloudy. Owls look great on trees and bad in leaves—but don't worry about it. Everything is open to interpretation."

"Ooh, do mine," I urged, my cup her way.

She gave the other cup back to Judith, who mostly looked amused by the exercise. "All right, let's see."

"Ask my leaves if the Ellen you found in a tree was my aunt."

She chuckled as she squinted down into the bottom of my cup. "It doesn't work like that. All I can give you ..." She shuffled the contents around again. "... are generalities. And very few things you don't know already. Rather like fortune cookies."

"Or tarot cards?"

"Cards are more precise, if you know what you're doing and if you keep an open mind. But like most other things in this world, they're unreliable. They play tricks when you ask them to make predictions. No, when it comes to cards ..." She still hadn't looked up from the cup. "... you're better off selecting just one for a daily meditation. Or you can ask a spread for guidance when you're trying to make a major decision. Sometimes that helps."

"But what do you see in the tea?"

She took a deep breath and let it out in a sigh. "Very well, let's see ... an anchor, I believe. That's good, and so are these triangles," she pointed at some smudges that could've been triangles for all I knew. They also could've been teeth, or thorns, or flecks of tea that hadn't made it down my throat. "All in all, I'd say the omens are good for a positive outcome."

"Do you think we'll find out that your Ellen ... is our Ellen?" I asked, a smidge too eagerly.

She looked up at me quizzically, an honest question in her eyes. "Would that be a positive outcome? In your opinion?"

"Of course," I told her. Before I'd even finished the reply, I'd started second-guessing it, circling back around to that talk Judith and I'd had—the one about wanting closure and not wanting a dead Ellen. But Judith and I had tabled that conversation, and I wasn't about to rehash it in this woman's kitchen.

She was watching me though. Staring me down like she knew something I wasn't saying.

But Judith was no keener to reboot the previous chat than I was, so she said, "Yes, of course. After all this time, we have all concluded that Ellen Thrush is dead. She was declared as such, nearly thirty years ago. The best we can hope for are answers."

"You could hope for a body. You could hope for a stone."

"That's true," she granted. "But I'm trying to be realistic about all possible outcomes. I'm willing to settle, and I believe Kate is too."

"Like I said, I never met her. She vanished before I was born. I've heard a lot about her, but I don't miss her. I want to know what happened for the sake of Judith and the rest of my family," I added as an afterthought, but I tried to keep it from sounding that way.

Jillienne nodded thoughtfully. "I understand. After all these years, any information at all is something." She gave me back my cup, and upon hearing a loud noise, looked out the window beside her.

An enormous black crow was perched on the other side of the glass, its shiny head cocked to the side. It cawed again, loud enough to startle Judith and me for a second time, but our hostess only laughed. "Thank you, darling," she told the bird. Then she said to us, "Camille is almost home. Here, I'll start another pot, and when she gets here, I'll introduce you. You can ask her anything you like, I'm sure she won't mind."

CHAPTER EIGHT

CAMILLE VENTERMAN PULLED up to the house in a black '68 Falcon with chrome trim and swanned out of the driver's seat in a shimmering black and purple outfit with bright silver buttons. She had a mane of thick, wavy hair that had been dyed a vivid shade of magenta and skin as white as magnolia petals. She approached the house on black boots that were pointy from every angle.

She was happy to meet us and pleased for the fresh tea, and she told us a version of Jillienne's story that was a little less detailed than the one her sister had provided. She'd been younger, she reminded us.

"I wasn't that much younger than everyone else, but I felt younger, if you know what I mean. I was always running to keep up." She and Jillienne had indulged in another cup, while Judith and I settled for lemonade with lavender and honey. "I was only seven, and I was small for my age."

"Your sister said you were the one who let the cat out of the bag," I prompted.

She laughed with a touch of embarrassment. "Yes, over breakfast. I said something about the woman in the tree and her last meal, and everything went straight to hell from there. But I had to say something, you know? I'd been sitting on this terrible thing for what felt like months—"

"But it was only two weeks," Jillienne interrupted with a finger held aloft.

"Practically a year, when you're in first grade."

"First grade hadn't started yet. You were fresh out of kindergarten."

"That's right, that's right." A wrist full of fragile, bright bangles chimed as she raised her cup again. One thoughtful sip later, she said, "I'd been having these dreams ... lovely dreams and terrible dreams, one after another. Sometimes they overlapped, and they were so loud that I'd lie in bed and cover my ears and shut my eyes as tight as I could—but it didn't matter. Awake or asleep, the dreams came anyway."

"Awake?" Judith asked.

"Call them visions, if you want. I couldn't tell the difference then, and I'm not sure I could tell it now. In one version, the woman in the tree was reaching for me, as dead and decomposed as we saw her that afternoon. Her arms were brown and brittle, and skin flecked off when she moved...when she rubbed against the tree. Her eyes were empty and her hair came out in clumps.

"Sometimes another woman would appear and shoo her away. The other woman knew it frightened me, and she was trying to tell me that I shouldn't be afraid—that the ghost didn't mean any harm and that she was only confused.

"The funny thing is, I figured out who she was. Not the tree woman, but the whispering woman, that is."

My voice was tight when I asked, "The whispering woman?"

"I'm sorry, I should've said—this other woman, she always whispered. I don't know if the woman from the tree was a proper ghost or not, but the whispering woman was definitely a spirit of some sort. I'd bet my life on it, and my afterlife too."

Jillienne brightened. "That's right. Goodness, I haven't thought about her in ages. It was the younger Miss Barlow, wasn't it?"

"Meredith, that was her name. I didn't know who she was for years, but when I saw a photo at school, I recognized her immediately." She set down her cup with a clink and a jingle and folded her hands. "Some teacher or another had staged a local history display in the hallway where the glass trophy cases go. It was all about early settlers in Hamilton County, and there was a photo of the Barlows—

the family with all the railroad holdings around here, and, and ..."
She snapped her fingers until she found what she was hunting for.
"They built that hotel, the Rockford."

Judith nodded and said, "Oh yes—that's where we're staying.
There's a large painting of Victoria Barlow in the lobby, but no sign
of a Meredith. Didn't she commit suicide?" She'd already told me
about it, but she liked to pretend otherwise and ask, in case any new
nugget of information was to appear in a fresh explanation. "I read
something along those lines."

The sisters shared a look.

Jillienne said, "Hmm ... well, that's up for debate. Meredith
Barlow had a history of mental health difficulties, that's no secret.
And when she drowned in the river, everyone assumed she'd done
it herself. But really, there was no evidence either way."

"I asked her once," Camille said brightly. "Through a board,
when Liana and I were up late, in high school. You were away at
college," she said to her sister.

"I remember. You told me about it later," Jillienne replied, with a
vague tone of displeasure.

She leaned in and mock-whispered, "Jilly doesn't approve of
spirit boards."

"They're not harmless. They're not to be handled frivolously."

Camille sat back again. "I know, and we didn't. But we had
questions and we asked them. Meredith said that her death wasn't a
suicide, so much as a sacrifice. She didn't care to explain herself
further, I'm afraid, even though we begged her to. Sometimes I have
better luck than others when I ask the dead for a chat."

"My sister is quite sensitive," Jillienne explained, leaning on the
word for emphasis.

"Only a bit," she protested modestly. "I pay attention, that's all it
is. Now Liana ... she's the real spook whisperer of the house. She's
friends with more dead people than living ones."

I was disappointed to learn that Liana was away on business in
Chattanooga, but the Venterman sisters suggested that we should
come back tomorrow. She was due to arrive around lunchtime after
a meeting at the historical society.

Camille explained, "She's helping them organize a haunted
cemetery tour at a graveyard on the edge of the city. It's one of the

largest in the state and it's chock full of historic dignitaries. Every year, the city throws a 'living history' event each weekend in October. It's a Halloween thing, and a fundraiser for some preservation charity or another."

Jillienne added, "Liana is a historic accuracy consultant. Her job is partly research, and partly asking the ghosts how to get things right."

"If she's not happy with the actors' costumes, she calls me in for backup," her sister said. "I made everything I'm wearing, and half the wedding dresses for ten miles around Cinderwich."

"Camille gets most of her work from the internet. We inherited a little money when our mother died, and our needs are minimal, but we each have a small income stream to add to the household pool."

Camille said, "My studio is in the attic. Would you like to see it?"

We swiftly accepted a quick tour of the grand old house, which had been built in 1869 by a cousin of the Barlow family. It was a regular funhouse of a place, bigger on the inside than the outside, or that's what you'd swear if you walked around it for half an hour.

It was a veritable TARDIS museum, I observed out loud at one point, and both Jillienne and Camille laughed.

I was relieved. I hadn't meant to use my Outside Voice, and when I heard myself, I thought they might be put off by the comparison. Far from it, in fact, Jillienne took the opportunity to show me a stash of Dr. Who themed perfume oils and a stained-glass reproduction of the vehicle in question. It hung in a bedroom window, catching the afternoon sun and sending blue-heavy prisms gleaming against the four-poster bed, the hodge-podge of dark vintage furniture, and the thick gray shag rug that was occupied by a large, elderly black cat.

I don't know if it was a boy or girl. The only attention it paid me was a soft meow when it feared I might step on it. Our hostesses mentioned a second and third cat, but they were lost somewhere in the mansion.

In the end, we thanked the Venterman sisters for their time and vowed to return tomorrow or the next day in search of Liana, who would surely have a third version of the family story. But it was growing late, and we didn't want to overstay any welcome—even though I could've long and merrily frolicked in the tasteful gothic wonderland the women had created for themselves.

"I think I want to be Jillienne Venterman when I grow up," I told Judith as we made the short drive back to town.

"You can't be serious."

"Why not? What's not to love?" I came to a four-way stop and turned on my blinker, even though there wasn't another car for half a mile. Old habits, and so forth. "She's got a killer style, a gorgeous house filled with tea and incense and cats and her sisters—"

"You'd sooner die than live in a house with any given member of your own family. Regardless of the house. Even if it was a Haunted Mansion version of the TARDIS, as you so astutely pointed out."

"Fair point, but lots of people get along better with their relatives than I do. And Liana isn't a blood relation; she's chosen family. I could live with chosen family."

"Like whom?"

The question felt a little sharper than she probably meant for it to, or that's what I told myself while I was sitting there not answering her. "I don't know," I caved. "Maybe that's why I'm so charmed by it all—because I don't have anyone so close, who I trust so well or get along with so nicely. You're entirely right though. I'd rather slit my wrists with a spork than move back home to live with anybody there."

"Home is where, when you have to go there, they have to take you. Or something like that."

"What?" I asked as I hit the roundabout that would take us past the courthouse. "What's that supposed to mean?"

"Ask Robert Frost. It's a quote of his. Or if not a quote, a solid paraphrase."

"A paraphrase?" I asked, feigning that I was scandalized. "That's awfully imprecise of you. You used to be much too anal for mere approximations."

"Yes, well. It's been decades since I was compelled by course-work to study the man, and I'll be damned if I'll reread him in my downtime. You made me think of him, that's all. That one line from that one poem. It's about a man going home to die if I remember right."

"That's what I reminded you of?"

"The bit about going home, yes." She glanced out the window and saw the diner. Before I could say anything, she changed the subject. "Oh God, not the diner again. It was fine ... it wasn't terrible or anything I just ..."

"The heartburn hit you too?"

"There aren't enough Rolaids."

"In your purse?" I teased, for if the Venterman house was a TARDIS house, Judith's purse was a TARDIS purse. She could've pulled a campfire out of that thing and it wouldn't have shocked me.

"In the world," she clarified. She looked up and down the street, seeking some other watering hole where we could carb-load for the evening.

"Not sure what that leaves us with. Want to do the Waffle House again?"

She did not look especially enthused when she nodded. "Unless you can think of anything else."

"There are a couple of hotels off the interstate nearby. I'm sure they have filthy bar food in their filthy restaurants."

"Waffle House will be fine," she said, not firmly enough to convince herself, but firmly enough to make me start driving that direction.

"Maybe we'll see something else on the way. Holler if you spy something you like, or something you want to take a chance on. I'm not above an adventure pick."

Judith was above an adventure pick.

We went with the ol' tried-and-true House of Waffles, and I got to watch her eat scrambled eggs with a knife and fork. I almost gave her a little hassle about having breakfast for supper—which wasn't like her at all—but it'd been a weird day, so I didn't. It'd been a couple of weird days, really.

"You know what I've been thinking," I said around a sip of coffee. "About the ribbons and the ... the stuff like a clootie well, but it's like ..."

"Like it's a clootie tree. It's strange, isn't it?"

I nodded and put the mug down. "Yeah, but you know what's stranger? There were already ribbons out there when the girls found the body. Who else knew she was there?"

She shrugged. "Maybe no one. The girls didn't see the corpse right away; maybe other people didn't either."

"Then why leave the ribbons? Why make wishes? What is it about that spot—that tree—that made it holy, if not for the body in it?"

She stared across the table at me, or through me. Then she shrugged. "Which came first, the body or the grave? That's the question, isn't it. Did someone leave her body there because it was a special place, or did it become a special place because she was there?"

"Right. That's what I'm asking."

"Ask somebody else," she said, more sleepy than bitchy. "Then tackle the whole 'chicken-and-egg' question, while you're at it."

It wasn't quite dark when we made it back to the Rockford hotel, but we were both so tired (and so full of greasy food) that it felt close to midnight.

We pulled in, parked, and headed inside like a couple of kids who'd pulled an all-nighter before a test—dragging our feet, rubbing our eyes. Anne was behind the counter again, and she told us hello. Judith had a message, apparently, so she went up to the counter to collect it.

I stayed at the lobby's edge, staring up at the painting of Victoria Barlow. "Forever pinched and dour," I muttered. I think I was quoting something, but I'm not Judith. I can't call the poet immediately to mind at a whim.

The woman glared down at me from her spot above the mantle. She appeared to be dressed in widow's weeds. I don't know why I only noticed it right then: her clothes plain and black, her jewelry the same.

Judith called over her shoulder. "Shall we call it a night?"

"Yeah. Except … come here, would you? Just for a second."

She joined me. "Yes?" She was looking up at the painting, same as me. Victoria Barlow had such gravity that nothing could escape her. Not even Judith.

"I'm a little rusty with my mourning fashion. What do you see when you look at the gloomy Ms. Barlow?"

She bent an eyebrow at the painting. "Oh, you're right. She is wearing mourning garb."

"For whom? Was she married?"

"No, I don't think so. Her sister?" she guessed. "Someone close, by the looks of it. She's wearing flat black, so the dress is probably bombazine ... or no. More likely it's paramatta silk. It's not shiny, that's why rich mourners liked it. The earrings are jet; the brooch is too. The cuffs and collars are crepe. But ..." she murmured, in a tone that suggested she was changing her mind. "That comb in her hair —it's an early mantilla style, and I think ... I think it's brown. Maybe gutta percha. She's about to turn the corner in her mourning journey. Why, next thing you know, she'd be wearing mauve."

It was coming back to me in bits and pieces. "Slighting the mourning."

"That's what they called it, yes—when a family began to emerge from the formal grieving process. There were so many rules, so many fiddly particulars. Mourning periods varied according to who died, and the family relation, and everything else. It was all a tad preposterous."

I went ahead and argued with her, for fun as much as a difference of opinion. "It wasn't preposterous at all. All those rules were just a handbook for grieving—they gave people a template for their behavior during a difficult time. Mourners knew what to do, and how to act, and how to signal their distress to others, so they could be treated accordingly."

I do believe she rolled her eyes at me, but she did it quickly and while simultaneously looking away. "Dearest, you're talking about capitalism at its most cynical. It was broadly considered bad luck to hang on to mourning clothes or baubles. You were expected to go buy a whole new suite of everything, every time anybody died. The mourning industry was exactly that: an industry. It was just a means of selling expensive social gear to widows and orphans—or their fathers, as often as women died in childbirth. And of course, it was easier for men. A hatband here, a bleak cravat there ..."

"'Tis the way of the world."

"Come on dear, let's go. I'd like to freshen up," she informed me.

"Freshen up? For what? For bedtime?"

She turned away and set off for the hallway that would lead her to our room. "I've got a different idea now. You've inspired me with your talk of dive bars."

"I have?" I fell into step behind her and caught up before we passed the stairs.

Back in the room, she held up an envelope. "Dive bars, libraries, whatever. Oh wait—the library will be closing soon, won't it?"

"I assume." I couldn't imagine that the little local branch would be open past eight o'clock, and we were almost there. The light outside arrived at a sharp, gold slant, the kind that said afternoon was winding down in earnest.

"That's too bad. I could use a place with better internet than what they have here."

I threw it out there, knowing she would throw it right back: "There's always Waffle House."

"Stop it. Just stop with the Waffle House. I can't even think of going back there right now."

"Don't disrespect the yellow and brown."

With half a smile she said, "I intended no disrespect whatsoever; it's a fine establishment that smells like coffee and grease and the kind of Neanderthal who puts a slice of cheese on a piece of apple pie. I've spent quite enough time there today, and I'm sure I'll be seeing those vinyl booths again before our trip is over, but let's space it out a bit."

"As you wish, madam. Hey, what have you got there?" It finally occurred to me to ask. "Who's leaving you envelopes at the Rockford? Who else knows you're here?"

She sat on the edge of the bed and opened the envelope, shaking its contents onto the quilt. "Several people know I'm here. This is from my grad assistant, Melody."

"I thought you weren't teaching this summer. Didn't you tell me that?"

"I'm not, though I don't recall telling you one way or the other. Melody and I are friends outside the hallowed halls of the university. She's been helping me research Cinderwich and the case of the unknown Ellen in between her own studies. It's really quite gracious of her, considering."

I felt the weirdest pang of jealousy. It was illogical and stupid, and I knew it—but that didn't make it go away, so I nursed it like a grudge. Someone else knew about this Ellen. Our Ellen, mine and

Judith's. Not the long-dead lady who'd wound up stuffed in a blackgum tree. (I couldn't yet imagine that they were the same.)

Ellen was supposed to be a private thing between us, or that's what I'd always thought. Or did I assume? I shouldn't have assumed. Ellen didn't belong to me. She didn't belong to Judith either, and Judith could share her own history with whoever she wanted.

I cleared my throat like it would shake the sour taste of jealousy loose, but it didn't. "So … what'd she send you?"

"Mostly, it's the paperwork for a conference I'm doing next month. In this day and age, can you imagine—an event without an online form?"

"Philistines," I accused.

"Hard copy only, to be returned by mail. Or I could always fax it all back, if I can find a time machine and locate such a device. Anyway, I told her to go ahead and overnight the forms along when they arrived at my office. That's what most of this is about."

"Most of it? What about the rest?"

"The rest …" She sorted through the papers, putting some back in the envelope and holding a couple in her hands. "I had a hunch the other day, and I asked her to chase it down for me. I keep feeling like the railroad has something to do with this whole mystery, and I can't put my finger on why. I can't find the bit of connecting tissue that ties it all together."

"Are you sure there's any connecting tissue to be found?" I sat down on the edge of my own bed.

"No, not yet. That's the problem. But Cinderwich wouldn't exist without the railroad, and it barely exists at all now that the trains have gone." Judith was staring off into space while she spoke, a sure sign that she was in full blown Thinking Mode. "The graffiti usually occurs at, or near, the old train station; the town itself was built almost entirely by a single railroad family, and back when the Cinderwich Ellen was found, broad public speculation suggested that she'd ridden in on the rails like some kind of lady hobo."

"Why would anyone think that?"

"Because no one in the vicinity knew her. She definitely wasn't from Cinderwich, and if she was missing from anyplace within a hundred miles, nobody had reported her absence to the police. She was passing through the area. Even in the seventies, people who were passing through were probably doing it by rail. I think the Cinderwich Ellen rode one to Chattanooga, and then ... hell, she probably hitchhiked here to town—or she was taken here by whoever killed her."

I frowned. "Wait ... didn't the Cinderwich station close up in the sixties?"

"1962. She couldn't have taken the train all the way here, that's all I meant."

"No, no. I get it. It's just ... why, you know? Why would a young woman find herself out at this end of the world, so far from home? What did she hope to find here?"

"That's the million-dollar question, isn't it. If it's our Ellen," she said, "it must've been tied to her studies. I can't honestly think of another reason why she would've come, though it's possible there was one. I'd like to think we told each other everything, but that's not necessarily true, is it?"

She returned her attention to the papers she'd left out of the envelope, but she didn't appear very impressed with them. "I asked Melody to take a fresh look at Ellen's notes and the progress she'd made on her thesis. I asked her to look for any connection to Chattanooga, to the rail lines, to the TVA projects like the dam, and so forth."

That sick feeling made my insides warm again. "You ... you gave her Ellen's thesis?"

"As much of it as I have, yes. I've read it too many times, dissecting every word, parsing it from every possible angle for decades. I've read that damn thing like a forensic scientist, and it's gotten me nowhere. I thought a clean set of eyes might be a good thing, so I had her digitize the whole stack of paper. There were only 72 pages of thesis, and about that many pages of loose notes in her files. If nothing else, I thought it'd be useful to be able to ... to search for keywords and make notes in the margins without destroying the paper. God, Kate. You should see it."

She was sagging now, holding the envelope in her lap. She let her hands fall there too.

"You showed it to me. We read it together."

"But that was a long time ago. The paper's all yellow and brittle now and some of the notes have been folded and unfolded so many times they're on the verge of falling apart. I'm trying to …"

I waited a few seconds, but when she didn't finish her thought, I took a stab at it. "You're trying to archive her. Or archive what's left. I get it. It's a good idea. You should do it now while everything is still intact."

"I hope so. I'm losing her, you know? I'm getting old. When I'm gone, I'm gone—and that's all right. That's how the world works. But I want to leave something of Ellen behind if I can. You know what?" she said suddenly, changing gears with her tone and the subject alike. "I'm going to put you and Melody in touch. If anything happens to me, she's the one you'll need to reach if you ever want to collect Ellen's things."

"Her things? How much did she leave behind? Other than the manuscript."

"Some clothes that are properly vintage now, and some shoes. A set of luggage. Some letters she wrote to me, bundled up with the letters I wrote back. It's not much, but it's something. You should have it when I die."

"You're being dramatic, Judith. Stop. I don't like it."

"We must be realistic." Then, more to herself, she said it again. "We must be realistic."

"Fuck realistic," I said, standing up and stretching.

"Yes, you would say that, wouldn't you?"

"And you would make light of it. Listen, I'm game for a dive bar. Hell, one of the hotels up by the second-closest interstate exit is a chain. Its bar might not be that bad, and they might have wi-fi. Come on, let's go. You can show me what you've got, and we can brainstorm about tomorrow over somebody else's booze."

"Yes," she nodded. "Let's do that. First, I ought to wash my hands and freshen up. Do you need the restroom?"

"It's all yours. Knock yourself out. I'll turn on the TV or whatever."

She rose to her feet and left the envelope on the bed. "You're a peach, darling."

"Back at you, Judy."

She disappeared into the bathroom, and I settled into sulk about Melody. Because I'm twelve years old on the inside, that's why.

CHAPTER NINE

JUDITH TURNED ON THE SHOWER, and I turned on the television, but I couldn't find anything other than local news and home shopping networks. I thought about flipping through the envelope she'd left behind while she was out of sight, but I decided against it. She'd know. She always knew.

I sat up straight, catching my eye in the mirror beside the TV stand.

My reflection and I looked out the window, where the pale gold light was turning a deeper orange. The sun was going down, but I still had ten minutes of daytime left and probably five minutes left of Judith being occupied in the bathroom. That would be plenty of time.

I let myself out and leaned my ass against the door to close it quietly.

It wasn't locked. I didn't bring my keys.

I headed down the hall and around the corner and out the rear door I'd used the night before when I chased the little ghost with white feet across the parking lot and into the trees. I say that like it was more than a hundred yards in total. I didn't exactly traipse over the river and through the woods or anything. Without the ghost turning me around and confusing me and leading me down corridors that couldn't have possibly existed, I made it to the small patch of woods in about 45 seconds.

This time, there was no woman with a shovel, swinging and scraping. No long-haired ghost with a pale finger held up to her lips. No lantern.

Just a hole.

The woman must've worked long after I saw her, for the result was pretty impressive. I crept up to the hole's edge and looked over the side. It was deeper and wider too. You could've stuffed a couple of bodies inside that thing, standing upright. At the bottom, a shiny pool of water reflected the tops of the trees.

I don't know if it was the well's bottom or not honestly. I have no idea how long the woman had stayed there, lantern and shovel, cutting a hole in the world. It could've gone all the way to China for all I knew. I looked around in the dying light and found a small rock. I tossed it down; it splashed; it sank.

I scanned the trees and saw the light from the parking lot peeking through. On the other side of that, the back of the hotel. No ghosts. No strange women. Just a hole that nobody needs and probably nobody asked for. What was the point?

And why hadn't I told Judith about it?

It felt too strange to say out loud—like if I tried to explain, she'd try to understand and quietly wonder if I'd lost my mind.

That's why.

It was still plenty warm outside, but the sun was nearly down, and a breeze rustled past, just fast enough to make me shiver. I started walking back toward the Rockford when I hesitated. I glanced back at the hole with its murky, wet bottom and checked the trees again.

I was still alone, but—

"Meredith?" I tried.

Nobody answered, so I went back to the hotel and sneaked into the room again before Judith escaped the bathroom. I brushed my hair and touched up my lipstick, and before long, Judith appeared, looking like she stepped out of an AARP catalog.

"Let's go," she declared. "I don't care if it's a Holiday Inn bar, but I need a drink that's made and served by a professional."

"You're giving the Holiday Inn a lot of credit."

"I know you brought some booze, but I want something in a

glass—not a plastic cup that came wrapped and sanitized for my protection."

I thought it was a little odd that she wanted out of the room so badly, but I wasn't about to fight her for it. "Sure. I've got my keys." I rattled them to prove it and stood up from the side of the bed where I'd been sitting, making use of the lamp light to make sure I didn't look like a clown in my fresh lipstick. I reached for the light to turn it off, then changed my mind. I didn't want to come back and find the room dark, for no logical reason whatsoever—if ghosts weren't logical. Of course, they weren't logical. Everybody knows they don't exist.

Even me, and I've seen one.

We left the room alight with the TV tuned quietly to local news and drove back toward the interstate. There, we did not find an actual Holiday Inn—I'm not even sure those exist anymore—but we found a Hyatt that had seen better days and a bar that probably hadn't.

We set ourselves up at a small table by a window so we could watch a whole lot of nothing go by while we drank our refreshingly strong beverages. The cocktail menu was short, but the pours were long. I was surprised and happy.

Judith didn't really seem to notice that her rum and Diet Coke was really more of a double than a single. She was restless, which might have meant any number of things. She was lying, or she was about to. She was ramping herself up for a difficult conversation, at least. My money was on that last one, and I knew I was right when she started chewing on the end of her stirring straw.

This was taking forever, so I went ahead and gave her a prompt. "Judy, are you okay?"

"I'm always okay, one way or another."

"Sometimes you're more okay than others," I pressed. "What's on your mind?"

She waved her hand, nearly knocking her drink, but neatly missing it. "Oh, any number of things."

"Well, why did you want out of the hotel so badly?"

"I didn't."

"You did," I reminded her. "Very much. Now spill it."

"It's such an unpleasant little hotel," she said sourly.

"Since when? You've only spent the one night, and it was fine."

"Was it?" she asked. "It smells odd. The lights are odd. The angles are odd too—all of them. Everything catches sound funny, and you can hardly hear yourself think, even when it's dead silent." She sulked down into her drink.

What the hell, I figured I'd swing for the fences. "Is it the ghosts, Judith? Is that what's bothering you?"

"No such thing as ghosts," she responded perfunctorily.

"I know, I know. But if there were any such things as ghosts, the Rockford would be ground zero for Spook City, wouldn't it?"

Something about her body language suggested I'd screwed up. I'd gone down the wrong rabbit hole. She was a little too eager to engage in a stupid subject, a little too fast to appease me by playing along. "You'd be hard-pressed to come up with a better … vortex, for lack of a better way of putting it. That painting in the lobby alone ought to be worth a good opening shot for a Tim Burton movie, don't you think?"

"I do," I agreed, but I agreed with a little disappointment. Whatever she was up to, she wasn't going to tell me now. "But have you seen anything that might, at a squint, appear to be a spirit?"

"Not at all. Nothing that couldn't be excused by the lighting, or the hour, or the number of drinks I've had."

"That's a terrible denial. Come on," I urged. "I'll tell you mine, if you'll tell me yours."

Now I had her attention, anyway, for the first time since we'd left the room. "All right. If you want to play it like that, fine," she said. "You go first."

For all that I'd been reluctant to tell her about the lady in gray, I'd been likewise terribly eager to do just that. Both sides had been balanced equally, but barely. One strong drink and a desire for something bigger than small talk, and I was raring to go.

I pulled out my phone and flipped through my pictures of the tree.

Slower and slower, I shuffled between them, suddenly second-guessing myself. From one shot to the next, I pointed at a gray smudge and said, "You see her, don't you? How about here? Look, there are her feet. Here's her head. Look at all that hair."

But upside down, in a dim bar, with my arm and neck crooked at an angle so I could simultaneously show Judith my phone and see what she was looking at—I was unsure. Maybe she was a pixelated blip, a fingerprint smear beside the tree.

"Stop it," Judith murmured, not taking her eyes off the phone.

"Stop what?"

"Stop …" She looked up and gently removed the phone from my pointing, clutching fingers. She held it in her own hands and adjusted the screen to make it brighter. "Stop trying to convince me that you're daft. There's something here. There's really something … I can see it." She pinched the screen to make the smudge bigger. "What is it?"

I was both relieved and twitchy as I watched her. "You really see her?"

"I see something. Here, this is the clearest one." She shifted her chair to sit closer beside me and turned the phone again so we could both see. "A couple of these pics, I wouldn't swear to anything more dramatic than a lens flare. But in this one, you can really see … her."

"You can," I sighed. "She's right freakin' there."

"I'd say that's definitely a woman, yes."

I nodded. "A dead one. Here, I don't want to lead you—not any further than that. Tell me what you see. Describe it to me, and I'll keep my mouth shut."

Judith made a noise that sounded like, "Yeah, right" muttered with her lips closed. She reached into her bag and pulled out a pair of cheaters, like she'd only just remembered she owned them. "It's dark in here," she complained and explained as she put them on. She adjusted the small glasses, set the phone flat on the table, and harrumphed thoughtfully.

"Well?" I pushed.

"I see a humanoid shape. A petite one, somebody maybe five feet tall, give or take an inch or two. Let's say it's a woman, for the sake of general likelihood. She's … barefoot, I think. Wearing a gray dress that stops a little past her knees."

"You're getting all that from the picture?"

"I'm extrapolating a bit, but yes. Is she wearing a hat? A very large hat? Wait, no …" she corrected herself. "It's her hair. She has quite a lot of it. There's something Victorian about her, isn't there?

Something about her shift dress, I think. It makes her look like she needs a candelabra and a dark basement."

I laughed, because she was right. "What's the expression? You don't see faces like that, anymore? You can hardly see her face though."

"That's true. I wish you'd caught her more clearly. I'd like to see her eyes. Windows to the soul and so forth."

I finished the last of my drink with two big swallows and slapped the glass down on the table harder than I meant to. I missed the coaster. "I've seen her eyes. Plain as day."

"You've what?"

"Seen. Her. Eyes. I've seen this woman in person. In spirit?" I was just a hair foggy from the booze and I didn't care. "I've seen her, that's what I'm trying to tell you."

"Where? When?"

"In the hotel last night, and then just outside it. I had a feeling she was hanging around at the tree, but I didn't see her there. It wasn't until I checked the pictures that I realized I was right all along. It's like she's following me around. No, that's not it."

Judith picked up her half-sipped beverage and leaned back in her seat. She crossed her arms and let the glass dangle from her hand. "Then what is it?"

"She's not following me. She's leading me," I said with all the hushed earnestness of a world-class drunk.

"To what?"

I sat back too, mirroring her. "Come on, for all I know she's leading me away from something."

"Do you think that's it?"

"No, because she led me to the well." Oops. Well, it was out there now, and I knew Judith would have a follow-up question or two. But she didn't ask anything right away, so I kept talking. "The well is behind the hotel across from the parking lot. I mean, I guess it's a well?"

"Not a clootie well, I assume. Or else you would've said so."

"Not a …" I thought about it. "… no, but it was dark. I might've missed something." Had there been any strips of fabric dangling like moss from the trees? Had there been offerings? I sure hadn't noticed any, but the whole thing had been so damn weird, I might've just missed it in the low light and confusion.

For fuck's sake, I followed a ghost out there. It was not the most straightforward and cleanly described adventure I'd ever undertaken.

"Think, Kate. What are clootie wells for? What do they do?"

"They don't do much of anything." The bartender slapped another rum and ginger ale in front of me. I didn't remember asking for it, but that didn't stop me from hoisting it up and taking a healthy swig. "They're places of pilgrimage. People go there seeking favors from the benevolent divine and the kindly unseen."

"Yes, people mostly seek healing, but they come looking for other things too. Fertility, favors—fortune."

"Clootie means 'cloth' or something like that, doesn't it?"

She nodded at me as if gently impressed that I was so successfully articulate, considering my blood alcohol level. "More or less."

"But I wasn't a pilgrim. I didn't bring anything to leave in the trees beside the well."

"No, but you were guided there by a force all the same— whether it was God or a ghost. Something lured you in and showed you a secret. It doesn't get too much more sacred than that."

I frowned into my glass. "Shit, Judith. Now I wish I'd brought something with me or left something behind. I feel like my manners have failed."

"Don't be ridiculous," she said with a soft smile that stopped just short of bemusement.

"Me? You're the one throwing around the word 'sacred' like it means anything to a woman digging a hole in the middle of the night." She opened her mouth, but I opened mine faster to continue. "And yes, I know you meant the non-Christian version of sacred, the version from interstitial religious practices the world over. The one that doesn't mean anything to Jesus, or anyone who prays to him. Isn't that how you used to put it?"

"That is, indeed, exactly how I used to put it. I'm proud of your memory, darling." She took a heavy swallow of her own drink, nearly finishing it.

I stared at her, openly suspicious. "Wait."

"For what?"

"You ... you didn't try to convince me that I'd seen something else or heard something else. You didn't propose a logical explanation for the pictures or for the woman digging in the trees behind the parking lot."

"Why would I do that?"

"Because you always do that. Did that. You always did that." I put the emphasis where I'd meant for it to go in the first place. "You: who teased me when I read my horoscope. You: who made fun of the gris-gris I picked up in New Orleans."

"I think you're wandering a bit afield from the original point. How many of those have you had?" she asked, pointing her eyes at my drink.

"You weren't counting? You used to count." I was exasperating her and I knew it, but I couldn't help myself. "Jesus, Judy. How did you and Ellen ever make it work with her interest in the arcane and your outright dismissal of it?"

She laughed at me then. She finished the last of her drink, briefly sucking a half-melted ice cube into her mouth, then crunching and swallowing it. "We had more to talk about than magic, you know, and Ellen wasn't so much a true believer as an optimistic skeptic. She believed in patterns, whether or not those patterns were immediately obvious. Whether or not they were anything more than coincidence."

It was Judith's turn to order another round from our new best friend, the bartender. I must have looked scandalized, for she adopted the most innocent look I'd ever seen her display. "What? It's not like I'm driving back to the hotel. Speaking of ..." She used her garnish straw to gesture at my hands which were clutching my glass.

"This is my last one. Swear to God. Or swear to somebody else, whatever suits your fancy." I made a show of downing the contents swiftly, that I might sober up all the sooner. I set the glass on the table—catching the coaster this time—and would've turned it upside with great finality except that it was still full of ice.

She grinned and shook her head with (what I hope was) mock rue. "We'll need a good hour at least, before we can hit the road and head back for the hotel."

"Thereabouts. I'm sure you can survive another hour in a Waffle

House-adjacent bar, beside the interstate, a few miles from a town that's hardly a town at all, and a hotel you've decided is creepy because you've totally seen a ghost there. Or you've heard a ghost, or sensed a ghost, or something. I don't know why you'll allow that there's a phantom in my photos, but you won't just admit you've seen something yourself."

"I told you, I haven't seen anything. You're the one running off on after-hours adventures without me, darling. Which reminds me," she said, swiftly changing her tone and reaching for her purse. "I was going to look something up."

"Something about ghosts?"

"Something about your ghost in particular. Shall we assume it's Meredith Barlow? I wonder if the internet holds any information about her." She called up a browser and typed with her thumbs almost as fast as she could type on a keyboard. "A few easy guesses and some educated speculation ... let's see." She'd almost trailed off to a mumble as she swiped around on her phone, slicing through the internet in search of something I couldn't see. The reflection in her cheaters showed me only flashes of light and color. "We'll assume she was about your age when she died."

"Why?"

"Because if she'd been markedly older or younger, you would've said so as part of your initial description."

"You must think I'm a hell of a narcissist."

She glanced up, looking at me over those small lenses. "Not at all. It's a very human thing. The first human thing, to be precise. It's how babies make connections to the world around them—starting with themselves. You're not a narcissist; you're tragically normal."

"Even more offensive, Judy."

"You'll always be special to me," she said, in the precise tone of a parent telling her children that she loves them all equally.

"Not helping. Not even a little. But I'll do my best to sober up swiftly." To this end, I flagged down the bartender and asked for a big glass of water, no ice.

Judith smiled approvingly. "Very good, thank you. I'd hate to wind up in a ditch beside the road. Or worse."

"Your votes of confidence have always inspired me," I said. Then

I made grabby hands at her phone. "So, spill it. Did you find anything?"

As if she'd forgotten, she brightened. "Oh yes, I've got her right here." She checked another thing on the screen and pulled up one more site as quickly as her data plan would allow—because we were well beyond the land of free wi-fi. Then she put the phone on the table and flicked it with her finger, pushing it into my space. It knocked against my just-delivered water glass, clinking like a toast. "I give you Miss Meredith Barlow."

The image on the phone's screen was smallish—a picture of a portrait that badly needed cleaning. It had the browned, baked look of a painting that's hung in a house full of smokers for a hundred years. This was a smudge with the face of a woman.

Hers was a rounded heart-shaped face with skin that was surely white as fresh milk without the nicotine tint. Her eyes were large and either green or blue, I couldn't tell which. Wild, dark hair was contained in a style I couldn't make out; everything around her face was too mottled and dark. Her lips were a tidy bow, pursed in a ladylike smirk. She looked like an art student's idea of a grown-up doll.

I think she was wearing a high collar and a brooch to fasten it. No matter how much I stretched and pinched the image, I couldn't tell what the brooch was made of, or if it bore another, tinier painting beneath her chin. It could've been a jewel or a locket for all I could tell.

"Meredith," I said her name. "There you are." Then, to Judith, "Her sister's standing guard over the Rockford lobby, but there's nothing at all about Meredith. How perfectly Victorian—to pretend she'd never happened."

Judith reclaimed her phone and turned it around. "This was commissioned when she was eighteen years old, so it's well before her madness and infamy."

"She wasn't mad. She was right."

"Right? About what?"

"About … something. The well, the—the digging lady …" I paused. I was too tipsy for solid linear thought, a fact that put me at a strong disadvantage when sitting across the table from my brilliant mentor of days past. "Does it matter? If she was right about any single damn thing and everyone else was wrong … we know what happens to women like that."

"Madness and infamy. Of course, if I died and everyone lied about the circumstances of my passing, I might hang around and try to set the record straight. It's a motive to haunt, that's what it is."

I hadn't thought about it that way. "You could be right."

"You still haven't said it, one way or another: Is this the woman you saw? The woman you followed out of the hotel?"

"Oh yes. God, yes. That's absolutely her. I'd know her anywhere, even, what—twenty years older than this? Yeah, I'd know her."

"Then why are you arguing with me?"

"Too drunk to stop myself," I confessed. "Wait. Are we arguing?"

She sighed at me and waved at my water glass. "No, dear. We're not arguing. Now finish your water. Rehydrate and get your head sorted out, so we can go back to the hotel and settle in."

I did as she suggested, but not without complaint. "Fine, I'll get my shit together so we can leave in a few minutes." I pointed one finger, right between her eyes. "But don't forget you're the one who wanted out."

CHAPTER TEN

IT TOOK MORE like ninety minutes for the water to clear my head enough to drive. Judith made me snatch my keys out of her hand to prove I was ready to rock, and it only took me three tries, spread out over half an hour. When I was finally approved, she went to the bar and ordered me a to-go cup of water that felt absurdly like a sippy cup. I took it anyway. My head was already drying out and feeling gummy, and the water would help.

The water did help. We piled back into my vehicle and headed back.

We didn't pass a single other car, not the entire way back.

When we parked, I glanced down at the car's clock before I cut the engine. It was only 11:00, and the world might as well have shut down. Cinderwich was dead and so was its only hotel.

The streetlamp at the sidewalk out front gave us enough light to cross the parking lot and get inside, and no more. There was a sconce to the right of the doors, but its bulb sputtered and spit and wasn't any help at all.

Inside, it was almost as dark as outside.

One small, low table lamp illuminated a corner of the lobby and a second one brightened the spot behind the check-in desk. Their combined efforts were wildly insufficient; I whacked my leg on a small side table and swore less quietly than I meant to, then went around the obstacle and into the hall.

The exit sign made the hall brighter than the lobby by half. It was safer there. I took a deep breath and let it out slowly. Judith visibly relaxed.

She fished her keys out of her bag. "Here we go," she chirped softly as if there was anyone else to hear us. The nice desk lady had said there were a couple of other people staying at the Rockford, but you couldn't prove it by me. I hadn't seen another living soul.

Once inside the relative safety of our room, Judith turned on the TV, plugged in her phone, and made herself comfortable. I took a shower, because I like to go to bed clean.

By the time I finished bathing and dressed in my ratty pajamas again, Judith was out cold. She'd put on her eye mask, set aside the phone, and turned the television volume down to almost nothing. She'd also turned out the light, which was fine. I could see well enough to climb into bed and grab the remote.

I was deciding whether or not to catch a late-night monologue when I heard footsteps outside the room. They were loud and coming fast. They were not heavy, but light and quick and determined.

Meredith?

I threw the blanket off my legs and grabbed my phone. If the more infamous Miss Barlow was back for another round of tag, then I was going to grab a good picture, for once. I swept my toes into my flip-flops and darted to the door.

I don't know why I thought it was Meredith. I hadn't heard her approach last time. Hell, her feet hadn't even touched the ground.

I took the knob and cupped it, hoping I wouldn't wake Judith with my, frankly, still-somewhat-buzzed shenanigans. I turned it fast but without any real noise and drew the door open enough that I could see out into the corridor.

Or I would've been able to see that far, if someone hadn't been standing in the way.

I don't know what I expected to find out there, but it wasn't a woman with her arm raised poised to pound upon the door. I don't know what she expected to find either, but I clearly surprised her, at least as much as she surprised me.

She froze.

I froze.

She said, "Um ..."

And I whispered, "Um ... can I help you with something?"

She opened her mouth, then closed it, and then took another swing at saying something, but I stopped her with a finger on my lips.

I cocked my head toward the room's interior, hinting that someone was asleep inside.

She took the hint, nodded, and retreated a few feet. She waved for me to join her out in the hall, so that's what I did, letting the door close behind me with the softest possible click.

She was about my age and height, with hair that was long enough to fill two very thick braids that had been spiraled artfully on top of her head—braids that were blonde enough to look white in the light of the exit sign. She was pale of skin and blue of eyes, wearing a long black dress with more lacey architecture than is strictly fashionable this century. She was a Viking who left her shieldmaiden gig to become a Victorian witch.

She said, or she accused, or she wondered aloud, "You're the woman—one of the women—who came to the house."

"You must be Liana," I guessed in a voice that shouldn't carry back inside to Judith. I hoped.

She responded in kind in the quietest murmur. I almost asked her to speak up, but she talked so quickly I didn't get the chance. "Yes, yes, that's me. I ended up coming home early, and I know it's late but it's a pleasure to meet you, regardless. Jilly and Camille had lovely things to say about you, just lovely, and that's why I'm here. Lovely people shouldn't stay in Cinderwich—they shouldn't come here, and they definitely shouldn't linger here. Some of us lingered too long and now we're positively rooted here. You know how it is, I'm sure. You know how secrets work, and how they catch, and how they keep."

She took a breath, and I didn't waste the opportunity. Quickly I said, "Secrets like Ellen? Do you know who she was?"

She shook her head so hard that I thought the braids might come loose, but they stood their ground. "That's not the right question. I know her well—I know the sound of her and the shape of her. I know the size of the shadow she casts here. I know her name is Ellen, but is she the Ellen you know and seek? I have no idea."

"Would you know her if … if I showed you a photo?" I crammed in another question. "Would you recognize her?"

She fluttered her hands dismissively, like this was all so much bigger than she had the immediate ability to convey. "That's not how it works, not always. Sometimes, yes—that's the short answer. Often, no. The dead don't always present themselves the way they appeared in life. Sometimes you see them as they saw themselves and the disconnect between perception and reality can be a vast gulf indeed. On the one hand, death doesn't really change people as much as you'd think; they're still the same lovers and liars and maniacs and stoics and everything else that they already were before they crossed the veil. On the other, they're free to be everything they ever wanted and everything they feared. They warp themselves around their ideas of themselves—do you understand what I mean? They're still who they always were, but more so and sometimes unrecognizably so."

Her eyes were huge and blue and terribly earnest, as if she hoped to God that she'd successfully explained herself, but strongly suspected that she hadn't.

"Okay …" I said, a little slowly. "I think I understand?"

"Good!" She clapped her hands together softly, then left them locked that way, like she was offering up a prayer. "Then you understand that you have to leave before things become unpleasant for you here."

"Wait—No, I don't understand," I protested.

Liana let out a tragic sigh. "I was afraid of this. My sisters can be … well, they don't mean to be misleading, but I think they really undersell the danger of pursuing …" She paused, rethinking whichever word she'd intended to use next. She tried again. "They've become accustomed to things here in a way that no one ever can or really does unless they've been here forever. They navigate the difficulties and dangers as a matter of second nature; they understand which threads to pull and which to leave alone, lest the whole world come unraveled. Not everyone has such innate discretion, certainly not people who've come here from somewhere else."

I felt like she was talking in circles. "I'm sorry, but this is the weirdest way anyone's ever told me to hit the road."

"I don't mean it that way! Not in so many words. You're

welcome here, of course. You're always welcome, you and everyone else. But you'd be well served to consider Cinderwich a—a game park, of sorts. Wear binoculars and watch the local flora and fauna from a distance. Take pictures and leave footprints. But don't touch anything. Don't leave the designated trails. Please, please, I'm asking you. There are forces at work that I can scarcely see, much less explain."

She came to the end of her warning, and the moment called for some response on my part. Weakly, I tried, "I appreciate that you've taken the effort."

"I haven't succeeded though, have I?"

"In making me leave, right this moment? No. I'm not alone here," I said, cocking my head toward the door, reminding us both of Judith, who probably still slumbered a few feet away. "My companion is older, and she can't simply be whisked from pillar to post. She's in bed, and I'm absolutely not going to wake her up, throw her in a car, and ship her back to Florida because a very pleasant but aggressively spooky woman showed up in the middle of the night and told us to beat it."

"Florida? Is that where you came from?"

"Me? No." But I didn't specify anything else.

Liana was quiet for another long moment. "Then this isn't your quest. It's hers."

She wasn't wrong, but I didn't want her to be right either. "It's both of ours. Ellen was my aunt."

"But you're not the one who came looking for her. Your friend is older, you said. She didn't want to make the trip by herself. She brought you for assistance, for backup."

"For company." I was only a tad offended, and I hoped she didn't hear it. "She knew and loved my aunt before I was born. I never met the woman, but you could call my interest … familial curiosity, I guess."

"Familial curiosity." She turned the words over in her mouth. "Good heavens, that won't be enough to save you, not if you trip over the wrong traps. Is there anything? Anything at all I could say or do to make you abandon this expedition?"

"Not for another day or two, but don't worry. I'm sure we'll run out of leads before long."

"What else are you hoping to see? What is the best possible outcome for your visit?" she asked, and the questions were entirely fair, if more than a little personal. If anything, I should've asked them myself, or asked Judith—long before we ever got here. They should have been part of the negotiation that had brought us together in the first place, but I'd jumped in feet-first, hadn't I?

I fumbled for an answer that should've come easily. "We want to find out if the Cinderwich Ellen was my aunt Ellen. That's the goal."

"But how would you achieve this goal? What proof do you expect to find? What conclusive evidence might persuade you that she was no relation of yours, or that she decidedly was? There's no body anymore. You know that, don't you?"

"Yes, but we heard there was a cemetery. She might've ended up buried here after all, if her remains never made it to Nashville. I know how people get lost, and how they go missing forever. I'm not crazy or stupid."

"No, no. I never suggested any such thing. You're right about the cemetery, and there was a portion set aside for those who couldn't pay—not a true pauper's field, but close enough as makes no difference. No one knows who's buried there or how many residents there might be in total. Not anymore. I could show you the spot of land, for all the good it'd do you."

I shrugged and told her the truth. "Honestly, I'd appreciate that."

"Why? I'd only be standing there beside you, pointing at an overgrown acre with few markers, or none at all. Without a backhoe and a DNA lab, it won't matter. Not to you, and not to your friend either."

"That's where you're wrong. Judith will never leave without seeing it, if there's even a chance that Ellen's buried there. Her Ellen," I needlessly clarified. "She's convinced that's who it is, and I don't know how much she needs to confirm what she's already decided is true, or to disprove it altogether. We'll visit the cemetery and the library, and I don't know what else. But we won't be here much longer," I tried, since that's what she seemed to want to hear.

She considered this and said, "Yes, the library. Oh my—yes."

"What?"

Liana was looking at a spot over my head, or just past it. "The spirits are in wild agreement about that. You definitely must visit the library before you leave. Goodness ..." she said, but it wasn't to me, or about me. "Will you promise me something though?"

"Depends."

She looked back down the hall toward the lobby, like she half-expected to see someone coming to stop her. "Don't go near any water. If you see a well, or a creek, or anything like that. Don't go to the river."

"The river's quite a way from here."

"It's not as far as you think, and the tributaries stretch longer and spread farther than you'd expect. Please, that's all I'm asking. Don't go near the water. It isn't safe for anyone, especially not ..." She stopped herself. "I'm sorry, I shouldn't have come. I've been rude, and that wasn't my intent at all." She was wearing a black shawl and she tucked it around herself more tightly, like she was winding up to a good flounce and disappearance. "Forgive me, and good night."

She turned to leave, but I touched her arm. "Do you really think you can take us to the cemetery?"

"I ..." She lingered. "I do enjoy playing tour guide."

"We'd be happy for the guiding, and you could make sure we stay away from any water, if that's so important." I tried not to think about the freshly dug well out behind the hotel and the dark pool that filled it. "Please? I'll buy you lunch, or coffee, or whatever. We'd appreciate your help."

She nodded and loosened her grip on herself. "I could show you, and then, after the library, your friend will have seen it all and you can leave safely. Perhaps after breakfast tomorrow? We could meet here, in the lobby. How about ten o'clock?"

"Sounds good to me." We muttered polite parting pleasantries, and she vanished like the ghost she could have been at a casual glance. I carefully turned the hotel room's doorknob to keep it from clicking too loudly.

Back inside, the lights were low and Judith was snoring softly with her hands clasped atop the fold of the blanket again. I got sleepy just looking at her. Then I got curious, looking at the desk beside her bed. It was the only one in the room, present for the sake of business travelers or merely convenience—who knows. It was covered with the small stack of papers that Judith had picked up from the front desk, all tidy and sorted.

I'm not usually a snoop, I swear to God. But I knew Judith too well, maybe that was it. I knew she was hiding something that she didn't really want to hide. She'd been wearing her inner conflict like a cheap cologne, and I'd given her every chance to unload. I even brought booze into the mix for heaven's sake, and I'd only succeeded in getting too tipsy to leave the bar in a timely fashion.

My head didn't hurt yet, but I could feel a touch of hangover sneaking up on me, so I went to the sink and got a glass of water. Maybe I'd buy myself enough time to remember that I'm not a snoop and snooping is wrong, and I had never snooped on Judith before. Certainly, I should not begin now.

It didn't work. Not very well.

I sipped and sidled over toward the desk, pretending to look for a coaster. I don't know why I felt the need for a cover story. Judith was wearing an eye mask—so it's not like she could see me—and the heater had kicked on as the night had cooled off. It sounded like we were sleeping beside a tractor. There's no way she'd hear me unless I launched into slapstick and pratfalls.

Maybe not even then.

Between the bulb in the bathroom at the other end of the room and a crack in the long, thick curtains, I had just enough light to see by.

I could see that her papers were sorted into three small stacks.

The first was made up of forms, clearly intended for that conference she'd mentioned. There were two Post-it notes stuck to one side, both with handwriting I couldn't quite decipher, but I knew it wasn't Judith's. It must've belonged to Melody, her new assistant who I was most certainly not jealous of, in any way whatsoever. I resisted the urge to pick them off and toss them into the little round waste bin beside the TV cabinet.

The second stack had maybe 6-8 sheets of annotated material from my aunt Ellen's thesis. This too had Melody's handwriting on it—right in the margins. No sticky notes or anything. A closer look said that these were just photocopies, but it still made me pissy in a way that I'm frankly hard-pressed to account for.

The third stack was barely a stack. It was two things, that's all: a postcard from Hawaii and a folded piece of paper.

I turned over the postcard and didn't recognize the handwriting I found there. The note on the back was a little hard to make out. I didn't want to stand there squinting at something that wasn't mine for too long, so I set it aside and unfolded the paper beneath it. It was a printout from a travel booking website, featuring confirmation details for a flight. Next week, Judith was going to Hawaii. She would leave from Orlando International Airport and return five days later.

I picked up the card again, and since Judith hadn't budged except to sing through her nose some more, I carried it to the bathroom where the light was better and shut the door. I closed the toilet seat and sat down on it.

The handwriting was slanted and narrow, and it made me wonder if I was starting to need bifocals. Gradually, I picked out what it was saying.

Wish you were here, but I understand why you're not—and I'll see you again soon enough! Good luck, dearest. All my love, Carol.

All my love, Carol?

Judith hadn't mentioned any Carol, but Judith had only mentioned Melody the day before. Judith no doubt knew scads of people I didn't, and it shouldn't surprise me to learn that she had friends, colleagues, and what sounded like a girlfriend.

Was this a girlfriend? Let's say she had a woman friend. Nobody named Carol was likely to be under the age of fifty, and the handwriting looked like it belonged to someone at least that age if not older.

Like I was some kind of expert.

None of this was any of my goddamn business, but that didn't stop me from having opinions. I certainly wasn't annoyed or jealous, not like I was about Melody. I felt something else entirely, and as I sat there on the throne, holding someone else's love note, I sorted those feelings into two parts.

One: I was happy for Judith. Genuinely happy, not reality-show-fake-happy. Judith had dated a bit after Ellen, because of course she had. If anything, her love life had gotten relatively hopping last I'd heard—back when we'd been in regular contact. She was an attractive woman with a respectable job and a house. "She's a catch," I whispered, smiling down at the postcard. But the other thing I felt—the second thing—made my smile a little sour: Judith hadn't told me about Carol. She'd wanted to tell me, but for some reason she'd felt like she couldn't.

I didn't like that second thing.

I resolved to make a point to bring it up over breakfast before meeting Liana, if we were awake in time to get any, or over lunch, if we weren't. I wouldn't ask anything too prying or personal; I'd say just enough to give her an opening to share, if that's what she felt like doing.

Now I felt a third thing: guilt. Judith didn't owe me this information. She hadn't volunteered any of it. I was really kind of an asshole, and I loathed myself for it. I got up from the toilet, turned off the light, and returned the postcard to the spot it'd held on the desk.

Judith was still a lovely corpse over on the bed. She hadn't moved a muscle, though her sinus whistling had changed key a little.

I tucked myself into bed and worried myself to sleep.

CHAPTER ELEVEN

JUDITH and I did not rouse ourselves early enough for a breakfast outing, but in the Rockford lobby we found a small continental-style setup that wouldn't have served more than half a dozen people. By the time we'd gotten dressed and out the door, only fifteen minutes remained before we could expect our cemetery tour guide, but I had a moment for a bagel and some fruit, if not any gentle conversational prying.

As for Judith, she was on her second cup of coffee when Liana swanned into the hotel, dressed much like I'd seen her the night before. This time she was without a shawl, wearing boots that looked like they'd be easy to walk in. She also carried a folded black parasol and her hair was braided in a single thick plait that hung to her waist.

"Good morning!" she chirped, but she chirped a little sleepily. Even small-town goths don't typically see the wee side of noon I guess. She extended her hand to my travel companion and said with a grin, "You must be Judith Kane. I'm Liana Heeble, auxiliary sister to the Ventermans—to be deployed in case of emergency."

I didn't remember telling her Judith's name. One of her sisters must've filled her in.

I'd already warned Judith about the previous night's encounter so she'd know what to expect. I think she was still a little surprised and I'm not sure why. It's not like she hadn't met the other two women for crying out loud. Charmingly Weird was the family brand.

"It's a pleasure to meet you," she said with all her usual graciousness. "I'm sorry I missed you last night, but it's just as well that I slept through your visit. We'd had a few drinks at a bar near the interstate, and I badly needed my beauty rest."

"You both look marvelous, and I'm so happy to have the opportunity to show you around," she replied, but she flashed me a look when she said it. She must've been wondering how much of her warning I'd taken to heart and if I'd shared it with my roommate.

I didn't give anything away. "Thank you. We're looking forward to seeing the cemetery."

Judith brightened. "Oh yes. You said there was a plot for the poor and there might be some unmarked or unmaintained graves. I can't help but wonder if the woman from the blackgum tree wasn't eventually buried there since no one claimed her and no one knew who she was."

"Well, anything's possible," Liana said lightly.

"Did Ellen ever mention anything about it?" I asked.

Judith frowned at me. "What?"

"She um …" I gestured at Liana. "Like her sisters said, she talks to ghosts. She told me she was acquainted with the Cinderwich Ellen, but that it was complicated. Isn't that right?"

"Yes, very complicated. I'll try to explain on the way."

"I can drive," I declared, but Liana shook her head.

"It's quite close—maybe three or four blocks, as the crow flies. Just outside the town square behind the old church." She snatched the last blueberry muffin from the table and held it up. "Anne?" she called to the front of the lobby. "Do you mind if I take this?"

The woman at the hotel desk shook her head. "Help yourself, hon. Everybody else has come and gone. Grab an orange juice, while you're at it."

"Thank you, I will." She did, and she looked up at the massive painting of Victoria Barlow, which scowled down at everyone who came or went. "Victoria," she said with a dip of her head, as if in greeting. Then she turned to me. "Do you remember what I said last night? About how the dead see themselves, and how we see them—or saw them—when they were alive? Look at Miss Barlow here." She pointed her OJ at the painting. "You see, I consider her a friend. But she looks absolutely nothing like that, not in the afterlife. She's scarcely recognizable. It's really something."

"What does she look like now?" asked Judith.

Liana smiled and headed for the door. We followed her. "Older, for one thing," she said, holding it open with her backside while we brought up the rear. "She was always something of a crone, even when she was a child. Have you ever known anyone like that? Sometimes people call them 'old souls,' and that's close—but it's not really right. She just ... never got the hang of being young. She would've been much more comfortable as an old lady, and it's a shame that she died in her fifties. She would've loved being an octogenarian."

Judith nodded. "She appears to you as an old woman?"

We walked alongside her, one of us at each elbow. "A tall, thin, bright thing. Her hair is pure silver, and she lets it all hang down. She always wears a simple dress, usually black. No lace, no ruffles, no bows. Not even a belt. She's matte and monochrome by choice."

"Then how do you know it's her?" I wanted to know.

Liana stopped, just long enough to look me in the eye. "Because I asked. Also, I mean ... you can see it in her face a bit. It's really an interesting thing, but I don't pretend to understand it. Now—shall we?" She pushed the door open with her hip, since her hands were full.

Judith was right behind her. "By all means."

On the way, Liana did indeed do her best to recap what she'd told me last night. As always, Judith was politely receptive, nodding and smiling when necessary and asking mild questions, here and there, as appropriate.

There wasn't much time to go in-depth because our guide was right: the trip to the cemetery was brief even on foot.

"It's at the end of this path through these trees," she said as we trailed behind her like ducklings. "Here's the old church."

The old church was definitely old, original to the town's inception—or so I should think. Once painted white, with great arched doors that were black, the small chapel's exterior had faded until the two were barely a shade of gray apart. The windows were mostly boarded, but half the boards had rotted or fallen off and at least one of the windows was broken. Several enormous, ancient trees loomed around the place, and two more had been cut down some time ago. Their stumps were the size of patio tables, mushy with termites and damp.

"Oh, what a lovely spot!" Judith exclaimed. "This must have been a beautiful building once."

"Still is," I added.

To Liana, Judith said, "Kate's always been fond of run-down places that are falling apart."

"True story." I pulled out my phone and snapped a few quick pictures as we proceeded around the church's eastern side. Maybe Meredith would show up again. Maybe she wouldn't and I'd just have some neat old pics of a church. Either way, I took a few extras.

The grass was high enough to graze our knees, and we collected seeds and tiny burrs at the bottom of our pants—or on the hem of her dress, in Liana's case. Judith swiped at them once or twice and gave up. No sense in tidying up when we were still walking through a veritable prairie.

Well, no. Not exactly.

There'd never been any grasslands on the acreage where the church sat alone. Around the edges of the clearing that surrounded it, the saplings crept in close, along with pokeweed, briars, poison ivy, and everything else that the forest sends ahead of its stately trees. Mother nature would retake it all in another few years.

While I grabbed a few more shots, I listened to Judith and Liana patter in the background and scanned the scene for any hint of a woman with wild black hair and tiny white feet that didn't touch the ground. But if she was hanging around, she was keeping to herself.

Did the church have anything to do with it? Consecrated land and all that?

I was about to open my mouth to ask our guide when she announced, "Here we are!" and stopped shuffling through the grass. She closed her parasol.

I hustled to catch up quick. On the other side of a small rise that could scarcely be called a hill, a smattering of gray and white tombstones sprawled in a loose grid. More than a few were all but illegible. But still, some held their names, dates, and loving inscriptions well enough to see at a distance.

Liana adjusted the sunglasses she'd pulled from a black lace bag and squinted across the scene. "As you can see, it's not exactly tidy anymore. At best, when someone was regularly maintaining the grounds, it was all rather wonky. The plots were supposed to be laid out evenly, but whoever drew the lines needed a ruler, I guess. Anyway, over here you'll see the Dewitt family group," she said, pointing toward a cluster close to the center. "And beside them, the Luptons. Beyond the Lupton family you'll see the Brocks, the Keenes, and the Wilcoxes; may they rest in peace."

"What about the Barlows?" I asked.

"Over there." She indicated a spot nearest the church. "Come on, I'll show you."

We dutifully traipsed behind her, falling into the building's shadow as we approached. One large obelisk rose up a little taller than any of us with the family name emblazoned in letters as high as my hand. Beneath it, a list of names. Beside it, several small stones set flat in the earth.

Liana was in full tour guide mode. "Here we have Richard Barlow, patriarch and railway man. Beside him his wife, Elizabeth, and his daughters Victoria and Meredith."

Meredith's stone was a little shinier than the rest and the carving looked cleaner. Her name was the easiest to read. I asked, "Why's Meredith's marker different?"

She smiled down at it. "Because it's newer. For a long time, she simply didn't have one. Given the circumstances of her death, whatever they were ... I mean, people thought she'd killed herself, and it wasn't the kind of thing you honored or remembered. But she's definitely buried there, right next to her sister. I've seen the old paperwork and map down at the library. No one would know about it now if Jillienne's mother hadn't bought the stone back in the 1980s."

Judith used the toe of her ballet flat to rub lichen off the dates. "Are the Ventermans kin to the Barlows?"

"Not in any direct sense that I know of. I'm sure they were distant cousins on some level or another, like you find in any small place, but neither family ever claimed it. No, Grandma Vee just didn't like to see her go unremembered. She was sweet like that."

"That was kind of her," Judith said softly. Then, as if she only just recalled what we were doing there, she asked, "But what about the graves that remained unmarked? Where can we find those?"

"Other end of the cemetery; as far from the church as one could get and still lie in consecrated ground."

"Wasn't there ..." I stumbled as I began to follow her but untangled my feet and kept going. "Isn't there some tradition about not burying suicides and condemned criminals in the churchyard? Why isn't Meredith over there?"

"Because no one knew for certain how Meredith had died. I think they were hedging their bets, if you want the truth. That uncertainty combined with the fact that the Barlows basically owned the whole town meant that their wayward younger daughter landed in a proper grave rather than a shallow hole at the edge of the woods."

"And leaving off the marker was another way to express their ambivalence?"

"They could surely afford a marker," she said. "A fact which says a great deal. I don't think they even held a public service for her, just one for the family. It was a different time in some ways, but not so much in others. They didn't want to talk about her. So they buried her close, but didn't take any great steps to see that her life was remembered or honored."

"They half-assed it. Gotcha."

Judith muttered, "Honestly, Kate ..." but I caught a glimpse of a tiny smile as she walked away, falling into line behind Liana.

As she walked, she told us, "Anyone of dubious death or unfortunate circumstances was laid to rest over here, in this general area. I'm not sure exactly how far the boundaries went—if you asked me, 'Where's the outermost grave?' I simply couldn't tell you. All I know, with any confidence, is that the western edge of the lot was reserved and intermittently used for those cases where corpses couldn't expect to receive an otherwise decent burial. I doubt very many of them were strictly unknown," she emphasized. "In a place like this, everyone knows everyone else. There might be the odd drifter or hobo who wandered through when the rails were still running, but the occasional stranger would be occasional indeed."

She came to a stop and we stopped too.

"And there are no … no …" Judith adjusted her sunglasses and surveyed the scene. "Legal records of interments?"

"I'm sure there were, once upon a time. The only records that still exist are somewhere in the archives of this church—a Methodist congregation, it was—if you can find them."

"Library?" I tried.

"Doubtful. Before the doors closed for good back in the nineties, the pastor and a few laypeople cleaned the place out and held a deconsecration ceremony. They took all the books and records, even the hymnals too. The place is completely cleaned out inside except for a little graffiti."

"You've been in there?" I guessed.

"I was a teenager when they closed up shop. Jillienne and Camille and I … we may have—hypothetically—let ourselves inside a few times to smoke cigarettes and drink Zima." She flashed us a bright, wide smile and a wink. "But if you tell anyone, I'll deny it—and you'll never prove it."

Judith returned the smile and said, "I doubt anyone would be excessively scandalized to learn that you three had peeked inside a boarded-up church."

"No, no. I mean Zima. Who drank that stuff for fun? It was awful."

"Kids who can't afford or steal anything better," I said. "As I might—hypothetically—know from experience."

With that, we officially ran out of banter—or else the scenery was getting to us. We stood side by side, staring out over the field with trees sneaking ever closer toward the stones at the edge of a shadow cast by a 150-year-old church that hadn't heard any prayers since the 1990s—unless those prayers were for better booze. The sun was warm, but the breeze was cool, and the grass rushed back and forth against our ankles. Beneath our feet, an unknown number of unknown people were buried.

One of them might be my aunt Ellen. Or not.

"This is where they would've put her, you think?" Judith asked nobody in particular.

Liana answered. "Somewhere in this vicinity, yes."

She cleared her throat. "And there's no way you could … ask around?"

"There's no one to ask."

"Really?" I took another look at the crumbling church, the creeping woods, and the weathered headstones. "Not a ghost to be found?"

Our guide shrugged. "If you were dead and you had the ability to wander, why would you hang out near your grave? Sometimes I see a shade flickering inside the church, but I think it's just one of the old ministers from quite some time ago. I've asked him his name, but if he sees or hears me, he pretends he can't. Not everyone stays with the same degree of energy, and not everyone who stays is very sociable."

Judith was a veritable statue. She could've joined the small field of monuments, standing there like Lot's wife, for all that she held very still and stared at something no one else could see.

I didn't want to interrupt whatever reverie she had going on, but I didn't know how to contribute to it either. Or if I even could. Or should. I kept the subject elsewhere. "He's like … a residual haunting? The ones where it's just a noise, or a scene playing over and over again?"

She shrugged and shook her head. "Oh, those are something else entirely; and don't ask me what, because I haven't a clue. They're not …" She went fishing for a word. She settled for, "…living, if you understand me. They're leftovers of a sort. Like the skeleton we leave behind when our flesh is gone; only another layer removed."

Judith came out of her reverie long enough to note, "Ms. Venterman said something similar."

"That doesn't surprise me at all. She's a wise woman and she listens to me."

We fell into silence again for another minute or two, showing respect to the unknown dead or just running out of things to say. We stood there together in memorium, Judith most of all. She was scarcely present, a phantom of a different sort.

Liana asked the thing I wanted to ask, but it might've been too much if it'd come from me. "Do you sense your Ellen here, Ms. Kane?"

"You said there weren't any ghosts in the graveyard," she murmured in reply.

"Ghosts aren't the only things we might sense. What do you feel when you look out across this field? Loss? Confusion? Relief?"

It took her a second to find a response. "I feel comfort. I think that's what it is. It's something warm and heavy, but only a little sad."

I felt it too, but I think I was only tired and overheated from the hike. I tried to keep from sounding cynical when I asked her, "Do you really think this is it? Is she buried here, in some long-lost lot?"

"I'll never know for sure, but I've come to peace with it. If this is as close as I ever come to ... to seeing her again, I have to be content with that. Maybe that's what it is. Maybe I feel content."

I didn't exactly believe her, but it didn't exactly matter. She could tell herself whatever she wanted if it meant she walked away with the closure she'd been hunting for so long.

I was opening my mouth to offer some agreement or reinforcement when I saw something from the corner of my eye. I quickly looked and spotted a flash of pale gray between the nearest trees. It was gone as soon as I'd seen it, but there was something else left behind in its wake.

"What's that?" I reached for my phone, thinking I'd try my hand at more pictures.

"Did you see something?" Liana asked mildly.

I almost said: A flash of gray. Probably Meredith Barlow again, that little minx. If I could've said that bit out loud to anyone, anytime, anywhere, this was probably it. But I didn't. I wasn't sure. "Are those tombstones? In the woods?"

"A few old ones from the main grid, I'm sure. Nothing from the pauper's lots." Something about her voice caught my attention. When I looked at her, she was fiddling with her sunglasses again and looking away, turning on her heel. "Well, that's all there is to see, I'm afraid. If you don't mind, I really need to get home. Lots of work to do. Paperwork for the historic cemetery nonsense." She laughed and it must've been meant to sound carefree. It sounded forced. "They want me to double-check some details on a woman who may or may not have been a practicing midwife or abortionist in the 1870s. There's a great deal of discussion over whether or not to include her in the walking tour, but she did great things for women's health, especially in the African American community, so she's absolutely worth talking about. No matter where you stand on reproductive issues."

"I want to see what's over there," I declared and started walking.

"There's really no need for that—it's the far end of the cemetery and the trees are catching up to it, nothing more interesting than that." Her voice sped up, and before long she sounded much like she had the night before. Not frantic but frightened. Insistent. Pleading to be believed.

I didn't believe her. I didn't think she was lying exactly, but she was flinging everything she had into the conversation to distract us, and it wasn't going to work. She knew it as well as I did. She could either keep talking or attempt to physically restrain me, and I was reasonably confident that she wasn't going to jump me.

I walked a little faster anyway.

"The original property stretched well past the tree line, and there also used to be … out this way, they built a little house for the pastor and his family, but it burned down back in the forties. The woods absorbed it years ago, but that's probably not what you're seeing. I'm sure it's just old stones."

"Great. I like old stones."

"I mean, there's nothing interesting on them, and you might even have some difficulty walking between the trees if the graves have become too sunken. You really shouldn't get very far off the trail here, for your own safety!" She wasn't quite shrill yet, but she was chattering a mile-a-minute, and you could see shrill on the horizon. "You'll break an ankle, and then we'd have to haul you back to the hotel, and the nearest paramedics are miles from here, but we'd call them of course. But what a terrible way to end a trip!"

Judith was having a hard time catching up; she trailed behind us both. "What are you doing, Kate? There's nothing out there."

"Cool. Then it won't take long for me to see all the nothing, and we can turn around and head back."

"Do you see something else?" Judith asked me rather pointedly.

"Not anymore."

Liana stumbled in her long dress and recovered on the uneven terrain with a few short strides. She was still on my heels. "You saw something else? A spirit? It could've just been the old pastor. I think he wanders a bit. Maybe he's expanded his routine to include the woods around the church. That's interesting—if you saw him too. Not everyone ..."

She kept going, but I tuned her out. Had she seen Meredith too? If so, why wouldn't she want me to approach her? Jillienne hadn't suggested that the ghost was harmful in any way.

Meredith Barlow didn't strike me as sad or confused. She struck me as small and wise and gleeful and mischievous. If she was a trickster, well, tricksters gonna trick. I could take it. But if she honestly wanted to show me something, I honestly wanted to see what it was.

I left the main clearing and stood exactly where I'd seen the flash of gray, beside a leaning tombstone that was almost as high as my waist. Two shorter ones were broken beside it, and I couldn't read the inscriptions on any of them. They were crusted with lichens and moss, worn otherwise smooth by the elements. Here and there, stones jutted out from tree roots. I thought I saw the corner of a coffin, but I wouldn't swear to it.

It was cooler in the shade. Cool enough that I wished I'd brought a thicker sweater. It was humid there too, unless that was my imagination. The place felt dank and alive, and not entirely hospitable.

I smelled water. Nothing fresh, not like rain. Like what you find in a birdbath after a few days.

I tiptoed between the trees, trying to avoid any stones or graves —as if I had any way of knowing where they were, if they weren't absolutely everyplace. I held my nose in the air, sniffing like a bloodhound. I found the well in half a minute.

Liana had stopped talking. I think she was holding her breath.

There it was again. There she was.

I heard Liana begin to gasp, and then swallow it quickly.

"What is it, Meredith?" I asked out loud, scanning the scene for any further hint of her. "What do you want?" I kept hiking over the knotty ground where stones and trees battled it out.

"God only knows," Liana said. To me, I guess. "If that's Meredith, I mean. She can be—"

"She's helpful," I said.

"She's unpredictable," our guide countered.

Judith asked, "But is she a liar?" We both turned to look at her. She was standing behind us, still in the clearing. Either she didn't want to dirty her shoes and slacks any further, or else we'd just outpaced her and she was catching her breath.

"I can't say for sure."

I nodded. "So that's a maybe, but probably not."

"How do you know?"

I didn't have a good answer for her, so I didn't try to scare one up. I just kept going until I'd left Liana and Judith behind me.

The well was just beyond the farthest teetering obelisk, a thick, sharp spear of a thing that was mostly held up by the tree that grew around its base. The hole was about six feet wide and deep enough that it was full of water about eight-feet down. Its sides had eroded, and the water was black with decomposing leaves and scum.

"What's that?" Judith asked. "Why did you stop, Kate? What do you see?"

"It's a hole, half-full of water."

"A well? A clootie well?"

"I didn't say that. Don't get too excited."

Liana hugged herself and shivered. "Stay away from it, please? It might not be safe. Let's go back. It's time to go back."

"Do you see any scraps of fabric?" Judith called. "Any signs of gifts or offerings?"

Did I?

I saw ragged tree limbs and rough bark, briar vines and poison ivy. The hole wasn't established with stones or other boundary markers. It was only an old pit collecting rainwater and whatever soaked up from below. But beyond it, I saw signs of other holes, deeper in the woods.

I turned around. "Liana, I've been wondering since the other night, and now I have to ask: What's with all the holes?"

"I'm sure I don't know what you're talking about. You found one, and heaven knows how it got there. Heaven knows who dug it, or why. Leave it alone—that's what I say—and let's go back to the hotel."

"There's one behind the hotel, you know—I could show you on the way back; we saw a woman digging out near the fire road when we went to look for the blackgum tree. So, I'm asking again: What's with all the holes?"

She sighed in surrender and began the short hike back toward Judith. She threw up her hands and said, "Who cares? For the love of God, just don't fall in."

CHAPTER TWELVE

LIANA HEEBLE LEFT me and Judith at the Rockford, pleading work excuses and offering polite apologies and promises of tea should we return to the Venterman house. She'd made clear on the return walk that she had no intention of saying anything useful about holes, clootie wells, Meredith Barlow, or anything else that wasn't tea. Tea had become the only safe subject on which she could be persuaded to ramble, and therefore, we parted company at the hotel. She hugged me goodbye and, taking advantage of the proximity, she whispered into my ear: "Leave this place, while it's still safe to do so." Then she held my shoulders and smiled a worried smile.

She hugged Judith too, but I don't know if Judith likewise got a warning.

"Maybe we should see about lunch," I suggested. "I could eat a horse."

She nodded, and I'm confident she was about to agree, when Anne behind the hotel counter called out to her. "Ms. Kane? Ma'am, you have another round of messages."

Judith had been looking a little wilted, but now she brightened. "Oh my! I feel so popular ..." She hauled herself out of the over-stuffed chair beneath the portrait of Victoria Barlow and went to the counter to collect a rolled stack of papers. "Thank you," she said, and then suggested, "Kate, let's take these back to the room. I want to change shoes anyway."

As it turned out, she also wanted to pick burrs out of her pants and wash her hands, which was fine with me. I used a fingertip to idly nudge the papers; she'd left them on the desk and showed no signs that she was feeling particularly private about them.

In fact, she called from the bathroom vanity, "Is there anything interesting in those papers?"

She must've seen me in the mirror. With that tacit permission in place, I flipped through them with a closer eye. "Melody sent some clippings. She says to check your email." Mostly, it looked like photocopies of old newspaper articles with handwritten notes in the margins.

"I'll do that; just a minute."

When she'd finished fluffing her hair and doing whatever else she'd had in mind, she sat on the edge of the bed and pulled a laptop out of her luggage. I didn't know she'd brought one. Before I could say so, she said, "I didn't know if I'd need it or not. I'm not glued to my phone like some near-sighted millennial, but I do like having access to the riches of the internet." She frowned at the screen. "Even when it's very slow internet."

"Slow and steady chokes the data plan."

"What?"

I pulled out my phone again to look through the pictures. "I left my computer at home. Me and Mr. Smartphone have it under control, at least for a few days at a time. But the internet here is sketchy, so I've been using my data plan."

"It's not that sketchy," she said as the machine booted up. She sat it atop her thighs and leaned back against the pillows on her bed. "I'm online now, and it's moving all right. Oh, here's what she sent. Let's see," She made a decisive click to open the email and read it aloud for my benefit. "'I've tried to do some more digging about this little town you're visiting, and I'm not sure if this is useful or not, but this is all I could find about the local freemasons. It seems the town was largely built and founded by a Richard Barlow ...'" She made some muttery noises to say that she was skimming through the things we already knew. "... blah, blah, blah—here's a picture of Barlow in Chattanooga, a few miles south. Not sure if it's helpful or not, and I couldn't find much documentation or explanation for the picture beyond what's written on it, but here you go."

She clicked again to open some attachment.

I climbed onto the bed beside her. "Let me see."

Judith adjusted the laptop, turning it around so I could get a look at the screen. Melody had attached a JPEG. The image was a black-and-white group shot on a pier or a dock or something. Four bearded and mustachioed men of yesteryear were standing around looking celebratory. One held a big jug like it was the World's Cup, and there was a cut ribbon sprawling across their feet. "Here, read that for me, would you? My cheaters are at the bottom of my purse."

I pulled the computer closer. The print at the bottom of the image was small, grainy, and difficult to parse. I gave it my best shot. "'Charles M. Lupton, David R. DuPont, Seth G. Coleman, and Richard A. Barlow, 1856, Ross's Landing.' If we're guessing that the names are listed left to right to indicate the guys in the picture, then Barlow's the one holding up the vase, or jug, or whatever that is."

"So that's what he looks like."

He didn't look much different from the other three dudes, really. They were all white men over the age of forty with competition-caliber facial hair and dark suits. If this were a police lineup, I could have never told them apart. "What are they doing?" I asked, not really expecting an answer.

I got one anyway. "Oh, hang on. Look, Melody sent another image. It's the back of the picture, I think."

Since I had the laptop closest, I went ahead and clicked for her. She was right. The next image was the back of the photo with handwriting that was markedly more difficult to decipher than the printed list of names on the front. I enlarged the screen and scrunched up my knees to bring it closer to my face.

"What does it say? Can you tell?"

"It says, 'Ross's Landing, 1856' ..."

"We got that much from the front."

"I know," I said, adjusting the screen some more. "Give me a second. 'Local Freemasons chapter ...' Okay, honestly, I can't read the number. Some local chapter of Freemasons, anyway. Local Freemasons ... something something ... ceremony on the ... completion? Let's say completion ... of the Memphis-Charleston connection. Then there's a smudge; I can't tell what's under it. After that, there's a bit that says something about the water."

I paused there. It made me think of Liana the night before, so frantic and demanding. Telling me something about the water. More precisely, to stay away from it because it wasn't safe.

"Kate?"

"I'm trying to read this, but it's ... chicken-scratch," I stalled. "Something about the water symbolically uniting the Tennessee River and the Atlantic Ocean. Yeah, I think that's what it says."

Judith pulled the computer back onto her lap. "Let me see." Like she could read a word of it. "I guess the water was in Barlow's big jug, right there. And if it's uniting the river and the ocean, then it must've come from the ocean."

"Or from the nearest well. Like anyone would know the difference."

"That's rather strange though, isn't it?"

I shrugged and swung my legs back over the side of the bed. "Freemasons, man. Source of a thousand conspiracy theories a week. Why do they do anything, am I right?"

"Sure," she said noncommittally.

"Hey," I said, standing up and cracking my neck first one way, then the other. "what say we go find lunch? You game for more diner food, or do you want to head out to the interstate?"

Whatever spell the photo had her under, the prospect of food snapped her out of it. "The diner's closer, and I'm getting hungrier by the minute. That was more of a hike than I expected, least of all on a continental breakfast and some coffee."

"The diner it is," I declared and waggled my keys. "Last one to the car picks up the check."

Before long we were seated back at the town's lone functional eatery (as far as I knew), going through my pictures from the church while we waited for our orders to appear. The phone was on the table between us, and on each shot, we expanded the screen to enlarge every fiddly bit, just in case Meredith Barlow was hiding somewhere in the background. We saw no sign of her anywhere, not in any of them.

When the burgers and fries landed in front of us, we mumbled back and forth around our food for a few minutes; we were both worn out from our (embarrassingly brief) hike and we were more hungry than chatty. But as our stomachs filled and the pace of our noshing slowed, I started a soft campaign to pry loose some details about Carol.

"So ... this is pretty much our last day in town, right?"

Judith picked up a fry with a fork and tapped it into a small puddle of ketchup. "Tonight's the last night I have reserved at the hotel, but we're practically the only guests staying there. It's not as if we couldn't stretch it another day or two if needed."

"Why would we do that?"

When she'd finished chewing, she said, "I don't know. I only said that we could, not that we ought to. There's not really much to see here, and if Ellen from the blackgum tree was our Ellen, I think we've come about as close to her as we're ever likely to get."

I slurped the bottom dregs of my diet soda, audibly signaling to the waitress that I could use a top-off. "We could tack on another day if you like," I said. "I don't have anyone waiting for me back in the city, and I don't need to get back to work for another week or so. Is there ... um ... do you have any reason you might want to wrap this up sooner rather than later?"

"What are you getting at?"

"Nothing," I lied. "It's been lovely to see you again. I'm glad we did this. We should do it again sometime. Knoxville's not that far from Gainesville. Next time, we could take a puddle-jumper between airports, or even drive it. You could come see me or I could come see you; we could take another field trip. Something less ..."

"Grim?" she suggested.

"I wasn't going to say grim. This hasn't been grim, really. It's been ... weird at times. But pleasant overall. We met some interesting people, we might have found Aunt Ellen, and I talked you into trashy bar food and drinks. But I know," I said, hoping the transition was as slick as it felt, "that you have a life outside of Ellen."

"I'm not sure what you're getting at." Yes, she was. She was starting to blush.

That didn't stop me. "Sure you are. You're a catch, Judy. A gorgeous woman of a certain age, brilliant and capable. No kids, no criminal record—all I mean is, I'm sure you've had other relationships since my long-lost aunt. And that's a good thing. You deserve to be happy. I want you to be happy."

I could've pushed a little harder, but I didn't, and I'm glad because it was just enough. She cracked.

She pressed her lips together as if to smooth her lipstick, but that's not what it was. She was trying to keep from smiling too broadly. She'd never liked to show her teeth; I don't know why. They're lovely. "There have been others, I just never discussed them with you because it felt disrespectful, even though Ellen had been gone for decades by the time you and I met. I'll always love her, but I've made room in my life for the living too. It took me nearly ten years to really … let her go, I want to say, but that's not what I mean, obviously. I spent those years in frantic search for her, to the exclusion of other pursuits. But time dulled the … the immediacy of her loss. Does that make sense?"

I nodded. "Sure."

"Eventually, I met Francis, and we were together for, oh, a couple of years, I guess. After Francis, there was Jean, who died of cancer back in the late eighties. Then there was a long dry spell, and a few others here and there."

"I don't remember you having anyone around when I was in grad school but considering the rumors—if you'd kept it close to your chest—I couldn't have blamed you."

"No, that was mid-dry spell," she smiled, lips tight. Ears turning red. "I focused on rebuilding my career for a while, and I don't regret it. After Vanderbilt, I toppled down the academic ladder and had to haul myself back up it again. And in recent years, it's been so much easier to be out than it used to be. Broadly speaking, if not universally."

The waitress arrived with a pitcher to top off my soda. When she was gone, Judith hoisted her glass of water with a wedge of lemon and said, "To kinder times."

"To kinder times," I toasted.

She sighed into her water and sipped delicately at the straw. She set it aside. "In more recent years—well, let me try again. Just after the 2016 election, I joined a group of like-minded women in a Facebook group of all things. Can you imagine?"

"You? On Facebook? No, and I'm mildly offended you haven't added me yet."

Her ears went even redder. "I only joined because of the group and haven't added anyone, really. Except a few of the girls, I mean. Some of us have become good friends in real life over the years, and well, that's where I met Carol."

I did my best pretend-surprise face. "Carol?"

"Carol. We met through the group, and before long, we realized that we didn't live very far apart. She's in Ocala, just an hour or so north of me. We met for organizing efforts in Central Florida, and then we met for drinks, and one thing led to another ..."

I couldn't keep my smile to myself anymore. I'm sure I beamed at her. "Judith, are you telling me that you have a girlfriend?"

She laughed nervously and picked up her water again to hide it. She was blushing all the way down to her collarbones and maybe farther than that. "Girlfriend. That's such a silly word when you're nearly eighty. Carol and I are women, for Pete's sake."

"Yeah, but womanfriend is an even sillier word."

"Very well, but you know what I mean. She's my romantic partner," she said with exaggerated formality. "There, I said it. It's all very new, really. We've only been seeing one another for—"

"If you hooked up after the election, it must've been a few years."

"No, no. It wasn't immediately after the election; we were merely friends for quite some time. We took a while to get to know one another before we ... we ..."

"Hopped into bed?"

"Stop it, Kate. Honestly." But she couldn't stop smiling, and that was a great sign.

I took her hands away from her water glass, so she couldn't fiddle with it anymore. "Judith, I am so tremendously happy for you, and for Carol too. She's a lucky lady."

She squeezed my hands and her eyes were bright. Not welling up with tears or anything like that, just ... bright. Happy, in a way I'd never seen her. "Thank you, darling. I appreciate it so much. Good heavens, you'll have to meet her one of these days."

"I'd love that. I'll buy you both drinks."

"Oh, no. Drinks are on Carol. She was an investment banker

before she retired, and she is quite comfortable."

"You've got a sugar mama!" Before she could protest indignantly, I picked up my soda again and made another toast. "To Judith and Carol!"

She relented, retreating from whatever objection she was about to make, and toasted in return. "And to old friends."

"Yes, yes. That too."

After lunch, we were both pretty wiped out, which says something about my constitution these days. But after the fire road hike and the church hike and sleeping in a strange hotel with ghosts and people digging holes, I was tired.

Judith was tired too, so I suggested a nap.

She quickly agreed, and so we returned to the hotel to crash for an hour or two. After that, we figured we'd hit the library, since it was the last thing on our list and it was the one thing we hadn't both done yet.

Alas, we underestimated our collective exhaustion. As soon as we hit our respective beds, we were out cold.

Two and a half hours later, I didn't so much shoot awake as gradually wander half-assedly into semi-alertness, groggy and confused. It'd been one of those naps that should've made me feel better, but it didn't. If anything, I felt worse.

Judith was still out and she was snoring. Not the soft, lady-like snoring of a prim elder stateswoman, but the proper snoring of a woman who'd been drinking last night and who'd eaten too much greasy food today. I loved it. I almost wanted to take a video, but I restrained myself.

I staggered to the bathroom instead.

It was a smallish, dim bathroom with two working bulbs in the light fixture and two more that had burned out ages before. Everything was brownish, even the towels and the tiles, and the sink had rust stains around the drain. It was a sepia room.

I turned on the shower because maybe it would wake me up properly, and I stood there a minute or two while the water heated up. I sat down on the toilet lid, which faced the vanity and mirror—hooray for watching yourself take a shit—and closed my eyes. I didn't need another fifteen seconds of napping, but I wasn't ready to pull myself together either.

I might have napped. That might be what it was. Surely, I wasn't awake when I stood up and went to the mirror and stood there without realizing it was a mirror at all. I didn't see myself, standing in a t-shirt and shorts, my hair a wreck and my makeup mostly worn off. I wasn't there. Not in the bathroom. Not at the vanity. Not running the hot water tap full-blast so steam would fill the room faster.

No, not me. Not there. Not then.

I was watching a movie or having some weird dream.

The woman in the bathroom glass was shorter than me by a few inches with a pale face and high cheekbones and the sharpest, shapeliest mouth. It was a full pink bow that angled when she smiled, and her eyes were so bright and round that she could've been a doll. Her hair was a crown, a cascade of roiling black water, curls down to her waist.

I tried to say, "Meredith," but nothing came out.

My hand rose to the mirror. No—her hand rose. She lifted it up on the other side of the glass and began to write with the tip of her finger. I didn't see anything. I couldn't read it. She was leaving faint smudges, that was all.

"Meredith," I squeaked. Her mouth twisted when I said it, opening just enough to let the word free.

I felt the cool glass under my index finger. I felt it dragging up and down, along in a line. I felt my own breath and it was cooler than the air around me there in the small brown room with the rusty sink and the 1970s tiles with odd floral motifs.

The hot water finally kicked in good, and steam began to fill the room.

Meredith stepped back away from the glass. She held her finger to her lips, winked, and vanished.

I was sitting on the closed toilet lid, my finger to my lips.

I put my hand down onto my lap, then stood up so I could turn off the sink's tap. But as the steam grew thick, it collected on the mirror. There, spelled out in the smears of fingerprint oil that otherwise couldn't be seen, was a message.

I PUT ELLEN IN THE BLACKGUM TREE

Shaking, I took a hand towel down off the rack and wiped the mirror clean before Judith could see it.

CHAPTER THIRTEEN

JUDITH SLEPT ANOTHER HOUR. During that hour, I did almost nothing but sit inside the bathroom and try to decide if I should tell her what had happened when I'd written on the bathroom mirror. Only it hadn't been me; it was Meredith Barlow. She was the one who'd written it. She was the one who'd been scrawling graffiti all over town for decades with the help of whichever borrowed body she could get her spectral hands on.

Or that was my theory anyway.

It was a pretty good theory too, since the handwriting on the mirror had matched both the message someone had slipped under my door and the larger messages that had been posted around Cinderwich all this time. It was Meredith's handwriting. Meredith had reached out, once by ordinary paper note, and once by phantom writing in a hotel bathroom. There you are—that's what the first one had said. She'd recognized me somehow.

Did she know that I was a relative of Ellen Thrush? Did that mean we were definitely looking at the right missing Ellen? I couldn't think of anything else that made any sense. She must know her in the afterworld. Or else Ellen must've known me by sight or blood. Somehow, she must've said something.

Why not approach Judith instead? Maybe DNA was stronger than memory on the other side.

But she'd seen me. She'd chosen me. She'd spoken to me, and I hadn't said a word about the note to Judith. For that matter, on the spot, I decided not to say anything about the mirror message either. I probably could have. Judith probably would've been publicly skeptical, but secretly thrilled.

She wouldn't really believe it though.

She'd whisper about it to Carol over drinks on date night. She'd talk about it like her horoscope, and I didn't want her to look at me like someone who made things up or someone who hallucinated when tired and overstimulated.

No, I decided to keep the whole bathroom situation to myself, even as I wondered to the point of distraction what Meredith had meant. How did she put Ellen in the blackgum tree? She'd been dead for years when Ellen went missing. Did she mean that I had done it? Not possible. The suggestion made no sense. I hadn't even been born yet.

Eventually, I took a shower.

I stood in the tub and let the water hit me on full-blast, high heat, and I banged my head gently on the tiles while muttering things like, "Meredith, you're killin' me here."

Then I got out. Then I got dressed. Then Judith was awake, and it was too late to go to the library. Come to find out via the 90s-era website it barely maintained, the place closed at 5:30. We could visit in the morning on the way out of town.

It was too late to do anything at all, unless she wanted to hit up the bar by the interstate again and get some more drinks because, fuck it, this was our last night in town. I ran it up the flagpole, and much to my frank surprise, Judith saluted. She was down to take another run at the interstate hotel bar.

"Seriously?"

"Sure, why not. What else have we got to do." She fished around in her bag for some lipstick, found it, and touched it up. "We can't see the library until tomorrow, and there's no one left to talk to or interview or … or interrogate, or anything like that. We might as well celebrate our … successful road trip."

"Successful? Is that what this was?"

"It's been roughly as successful as we had any right to hope. I feel relieved, honestly. I'm so glad we came, though I'm sure I'll never know exactly what happened to her. But it's something to know that she's really, truly, altogether gone from the world. I'm glad to have found this certainty, even if she's lost to time in every tangible way I can imagine."

"You've decided that the Cinderwich Ellen was your Ellen. Our Ellen," I summed up.

"I've decided that it was her, yes."

But that was a different thing, wasn't it? She'd drawn a conclusion, not found fresh evidence or a smoking gun. Had she arrived at this closure because she really felt something or saw something she'd chosen not to share with me? Obviously—even recently—I'd seen things I'd kept from Judith; maybe she was doing the same thing.

All the same, I was inclined to believe her, or agree with her, and choose to conclude that the Cinderwich Ellen was almost certainly Ellen Thrush, despite the fact that other people with other Ellens had surely come to the same conclusion across the years.

How many people had gone to Cinderwich and found their long-lost daughter, sister, mother, or lover? Scads, surely. The Cinderwich Ellen was a cipher. She was all things to everyone. Her details were so foggy by now that she could've looked like anybody, and we couldn't all be correct about her identity. She couldn't possibly belong to all of us.

But Meredith had called out to me. She'd seen me. We had to have Ellen in common.

Judith had to be right.

At any rate, we piled into my car right as the sun was going down. Was it too early to hit the bar? Yes. Did we care? Not remotely. I had decided to let myself be happy and ignore Miss Barlow's message.

Or internalize it. Or whatever.

We might as well get out of town, which would make Liana happy at least. I assumed—unless a nearby bar counted as a water source, ha ha—how big did a water source have to be in order to count as a danger? A puddle? A pool? A pint glass? Oh well. I'd take my chances if I could hold the risk in just one hand.

All in all, Judith and I were in pretty good spirits as we drove down the narrow little route that was flanked by tall trees and unmarked by much in the way of signs or scenery. The sun was thinking about setting and the shadows were very long, very thin. They laced together like fingers across the road, making it feel dark already, except for where warm gold light pierced through.

Here and there. Less and less. The farther we went.

But we weren't terribly far away from Cinderwich when my car started acting up.

It was old and paid for, but it wasn't a total piece of junk, and it didn't usually flash the "check engine" light for no good reason. For that matter, I didn't think it'd ever flashed the light in the entire time I'd owned it, except the one time I accidentally let it run out of oil.

Judith saw me frowning down at the dashboard. "What's wrong?"

"Not sure. The engine light's on, and it's running a little rough." On cue, the car coughed.

"Oh dear. Maybe we should turn back?"

I shook my head. I refused to panic. "Why would we do that? If the car explodes, we'll be better off if we're closer to the interstate. It'll be easier for a tow truck to find us that way, so let's see if we can limp it out to the bar. I'll call Triple-A from the parking lot or something."

No such luck. From under the hood came a sound like a spark plug in a garbage disposal, and the engine cut out altogether. The car bucked, shook, and slowed.

We coasted to the side of the road, finding a spot that had some semblance of a shoulder where I could pull off. "Well, fuck me running," I complained to the world at large. I removed the keys and reached for my purse in the back seat. "Maybe it's something minor and we can get it sorted out fast."

"Maybe we can Uber the rest of the way to the bar."

I gave her the ol' stink-eye. "Seriously? You think we'll find an Uber? I'm not even sure they have them in Chattanooga, much less this far out in the boonies."

She looked out the window at all the dim nothingness for miles around and sighed. "No, I guess you're right."

I hauled my purse into my lap and got my wallet and phone out. "I'll call for a tow truck and we can just wait in the car. At least it isn't cold."

Judith looked worried, but she sounded solid when she said, "I'm sure it'll be fine."

"We have a phone. We have—" I checked. Two bars. "A signal. And soon we'll have a tow truck. Worst case scenario, I still have that bottle in the room. We can have cheap brown booze in front of the TV."

"Worst case scenario," she echoed.

"Yup." I looked up the number and called it. The guy on the other end of the line said it was no problem. He knew where Cinderwich was and everything. He'd have a truck at our location within an hour.

"An hour?" Judith squeaked.

"It's only an hour, and it's not even all the way dark yet."

"It'll be dark in an hour. Sooner than that even. Look, Kate. The sky's going all purple."

I sighed. "The truck will be here soon, and it'll be fine. Haven't you ever been stuck on the side of the road before?"

"Not since it was safe to hitchhike home, no." She held her bag tightly in her lap. "I feel very exposed and vulnerable like this. I don't like it."

"Um, I'm not sure it's ever really been safe to hitchhike."

"Back in the seventies, we did it all the time."

I snorted. "Yeah, I've seen Mindhunter. Back in the seventies, you had a lot of hitchhikers, but as I understand it, you also had a lot of serial killers. Look, I'm sorry about the inconvenience, okay? This is nobody's idea of a picnic, but we'll survive."

"Don't talk like that."

I shrugged and looked down at my phone. "Well, we will. And now I wish I'd brought that bottle with me."

"An open container? In this state?"

"Is Tennessee especially hard on driving drinkers, or what?"

"I don't know," she grumbled. "It's just a bad idea in general."

"Which is why it's still in the hotel room, and tomorrow I'll throw it in the trunk if there's anything left. Will that make you happy?"

"The immediate arrival of a tow truck would make me happy. A drink from a bar would make me happy. A drink from your bottle back in the hotel room—even that would make me happy. Sitting in the dark, halfway between nowhere and the interstate in the middle of the night does not make me happy."

"Judith, it's not that late. Jesus, what time do you go to bed?"

"I'm not that old."

I leaned back against the headrest. "I didn't say you were. I was only teasing, I'm sorry. All we have to do is be a little patient. This guy will be here soon, and we can have him tow us to a shop and drive us back to the hotel. I'll find out in the morning if I need to reserve another night or two at the Rockford while the car gets fixed. Your rental should be fine though. You can still leave tomorrow and join Carol in Hawaii in no time flat."

Oops. I fucked up. I knew it as soon as I'd said it, but the words were already out there. Nothing to be done about it now.

Judith looked at me slowly. She narrowed her eyes. "What was that again?"

"I meant … um …"

"You knew about Hawaii. I didn't tell you about Hawaii."

"Well, I haven't known for very long. Please, I—"

She stopped me. "You went through my papers."

Goddammit. "You left them on the desk. I wasn't trying to snoop, I just saw the postcard, that's all."

"You knew all along, and you … you dragged it out of me, like I was telling you something you didn't already know."

Now I leaned forward and smacked my head gently on the top of the steering wheel. "I'm sorry. It made me happy to see that you were happy and I wanted you to feel like you could share that with me. I wanted you to feel … I don't know. Safe enough, I guess. All I did was look at a postcard that you left sitting out in the open. I didn't mean to betray your privacy."

She sulked. "But you did. You know you did."

I protested weakly. "You could've told me first, but you didn't."

"Don't you turn this around. Don't you make it my fault."

"Nothing is your fault. Yes, I knew about Carol. I still wanted to hear about her from you, but I didn't want to tell you that I'd seen the postcard because of this. Exactly this. This precise conversation. Or fight, if that's what it is." Still face-down on the steering wheel, I flapped my hand in her general direction. "I didn't want to fight with you. I should've just told you I'd seen it and asked up front.

But since you hadn't told me, I thought maybe you didn't want me to know, and I was trying to respect your privacy."

"Even as you didn't. Yes, I see what this is." She reached for the door handle and pulled it, but the doors locked automatically when I hit ten miles an hour. I pushed the button that unlocked them. She tried the handle again and the door opened.

Wearily, I called her name. "Judith, what are you doing?"

"Getting some air." She stepped out onto the shoulder and slammed the door behind herself, then leaned back against it. Her shoulders shifted around. I couldn't see what she was doing, but I could guess.

For years, she'd convinced herself that no one knew she smoked. When I told her that I knew—on account of I had a nose—she'd been so embarrassed that I never brought it up again. If she'd thought I'd ever glimpsed her with a lit cigarette, she'd spiral into shame and projection, accusing me of thinking less of her and pitching a fit. Frankly, it wasn't worth the trouble. I'd carried on pretending I didn't know and looked away if I accidentally got a peek.

I didn't think she'd had any cigarettes since she'd arrived, but I might've been wrong. She might've gotten sneakier, or then again, maybe she only kept a pack handy in case of unexpected stress. Surely this counted—this argument, this breakdown. This night. This town. This dead woman.

I slumped in the driver's seat and let her stand there, discreetly smoking against the car. After a minute or two, she stepped away from the vehicle, wandering toward the trees. I almost rolled down the window and said something, but she only went a few feet before she stopped.

The last glow of daylight was dying down and now the moon was coming out, not that it helped much. There were no other lights, not from any city, not from any public utilities. When the dome light in the car went out and my eyes adjusted to the lack of light, I could see Judith a little better. She was pacing, a couple of steps this way, a couple of steps that way.

Her back went straight and her neck craned. Forward, away from the car, she took a few more steps. "Kate?" she called back to me.

"What?" I asked from inside the car, with the windows rolled up. I don't think she heard me. She probably didn't hear me when I mumbled, "I said I was sorry," either. Then I pressed the button to roll down the window. "What is it, Judy? Is everything all right?"

Then she asked, like we weren't in the middle of bickering at all, "Do you have a flashlight?" She looked back at the car, but I could barely see her face. It was nothing but a pale oval in the dark, and her clothes were just streaks of gray, streaks of cream.

"Are you okay? What's going on?"

Her voice was tight. "I told you I need a flashlight."

"Fine, all right. Hang on," I said.

I unhooked my seat belt, which I probably should've done sooner, and reached over into the glove box. I popped the latch and felt around inside. I knew I had a light somewhere, I just had to find it. It was a pink multi-purpose tool that also had an emergency flasher, a window breaker, and a seatbelt cutter built right in. I hoped the batteries were still good. I'd never changed them. Ever.

I smacked it a couple of times for luck, then held my breath and flipped the switch. It came on, not too bright, but steady. I climbed out of the car. I stood there, holding the door ajar with my torso and hip. "Judith, here's a light. What do you need it for? What are you doing?"

Defiantly, she said, "I'm smoking."

"Good for you. But why do you want a flashlight?"

She pointed at the woods with her cigarette, the bright red coal showing the way. "Because I saw something. Over there."

"Trees?"

"Just get over here. Something weird is going on."

Of that, I had no doubt. I also had no interest in exploring, but she was insistent and it's not like we were going anywhere else anytime fast. Examining something weird together beat sitting in the car and fighting any day of the week.

"Is it somebody digging a hole?" I asked as I shut the car door. "Or are we talking about something weirder than that?"

"I can't tell yet."

I went for the obvious. "Is it a ghost?"

She hesitated, which surprised me. Then she said with caution in her voice, "Let's say no for now. I thought I heard somebody calling, and when I tried to look—tried to see—" She took the flashlight from my hand and pointed it. "I saw something moving. But then it was gone. I don't know what it was."

"So ... maybe a ghost."

"Only maybe. Do you see anything? It was ... over there. Kind of." She wobbled the light to outline a vague circle. "Is that ... is there ..." Judith changed tactics. At the top of her lungs, she called out, "Hello? Is someone there?"

"Jesus, Judy. Like we weren't just talking about serial killers."

"Someone might need help."

"That's how the axe murderers sucker you in." I hugged myself and shivered. It was cool now that the sun was all but totally gone. I didn't like it. I could hear something, yes. It didn't sound like a person. It didn't sound like an animal either. "What's that noise?"

"You hear it too? I thought it was someone whispering or gasping. But now I don't know." She panned the light across the trees. It showed us trunks, leaves, and not much else.

I theorized out loud. "I think it's running water."

"Water? We're miles from the river. And the dam."

"Something smaller then: a creek or a stream. There are a zillion stupid little tributaries ..." I stumbled. I caught Judith's arm and held it until we were both steady. I couldn't see where I was stepping since she was holding the light. "All over the damn place. We must be close to one of them."

"That's ... probably all it is," she agreed without much conviction. "But we shouldn't leave the car to make sure."

"Nope. We should definitely stay right the fuck here." My mind swirled with visions of serial killers and Liana's wild eyes when she'd impressed upon me that no one should, under any circumstances, approach any of the naturally occurring water sources near the town. I thought of the ribbons and the clootie wells, and the freshly dug holes and the freemasons, and I wondered how they could be blamed for this weird-ass town and all the awful secrets that squirmed inside it.

But whatever was making the noise couldn't have been a creek—or not merely a creek. There was more to the sound than the whispering rush of water on rocks. It had a rhythm to it too. A strange patter, like the flow of conversation.

Or not a conversation, but a monologue. A rhyming verse read aloud.

A chant.

No, that was ridiculous. No one was chanting. No river was running past us. We were frightened, that's all. I believed in ghosts because I had no choice in the matter anymore; but I refused to believe in anything else. Not until I had to.

In the weak yellow orb of the flashlight's beam, something moved.

Judith and I jumped. I clutched her arm again. She clutched mine. "What was that?" I asked.

"It looked like a tree. A small tree. It moved," she said, her nails digging through my sweater into my skin. "I swear to God, it moved."

Trying to be cool, I said, "It doesn't take much to move a little tree."

"No, I suppose it doesn't."

Her hand shook, and the light did too, its quivering exaggerated by the distance between her hand and the edge of the light twenty or thirty yards away. But you could see another slim wisp of a baby tree leaning, bending, bowing hard to the side. Then it snapped upright again, as if something unseen had just pushed past it.

It made a sharp, fast sound. The arc of a whip. The swoop of a fencer's foil.

Another tree. Closer. A sapling about the same size as the first two.

It leaned, nearly touching the ground, but not breaking. Then, with the terrible raspy whistle, it sprang back to a standing position.

The next tree. Closer still.

Lean. Stretch. Whoosh. Back into place.

"Judith."

"Kate."

Our backs were up against the car. It wasn't locked, but it wasn't going to take us anywhere either. "Judith, you don't see anything that's actually coming toward us, do you?"

"No, I do not."

The snake-fast hiss and snap was drawing nearer, and behind it —or driven by it—we still heard the rumbling whispers of the unseen creek. Something was large and something was absolutely unseeable except by virtue of its absence. We saw it by the leaning trees and their bending branches. We heard it in the grinding earth and the hushed rustle of grass being parted and crushed.

I asked her, "Should we get back in the car?"

She didn't answer. She held up the light, shaking but direct. She pointed it at whatever was coming for us. Whatever we could not see. Maybe it couldn't be seen at all, by us or anybody else. It didn't even cast a shadow, despite the direct application of the flashlight beam.

"Judith?"

"I don't know," she answered, her voice hardly more than a croak.

We couldn't just stand there. We couldn't go anywhere in the car.

We could barricade ourselves inside a Honda Civic that was almost old enough to vote, or we could make a run for it—an out-of-shape 40-something academic and a woman who would've been furious if I'd described her as elderly.

Whatever was coming, it wasn't moving very fast. We might be able to outrun it as far as town. Cinderwich wasn't more than a mile back down the road, I didn't think. Well, maybe I could do it, if I absolutely had to, but I was less sure about Judith. Even if she could make it all the way back to our hotel at a dead run, could her heart take it? Would she expire dramatically at the Rockford Inn? I couldn't stand the thought of it.

Judith may have had her doubts too, but that didn't stop her. Despite her obvious difficulty, she made an executive decision on the fly. "Run!" she commanded.

In all the time I've known her, I've never really disobeyed her. Argued, yes. Whined, occasionally. But disobeyed? I'm not sure I even know how. So, on her cue, I ran. Together we might make it back to town, or we might not.

Maybe the thing would lose interest before we reached it.

Maybe Judith would drop dead of a heart attack somewhere between here and there.

Maybe some car would come along and see two women running beside the road at night and take pity on us. Maybe it wouldn't be an axe murderer. Maybe we could do this.

We ran around the car and set off down the middle of the road, the flashlight bobbing wildly in Judith's hand, making the whole night look ragged and confusing. But we could see the road and anybody who might be coming or going could see us too. Hopefully they wouldn't run us down. Hopefully they wouldn't push us off the road into a ditch, and I'd sprain my ankle and Judith would break a hip.

All I had in the whole world was a fistful of maybes and a little bit of hope. It wasn't enough and I knew it.

Behind us, something reached the road. Something rose up, and whatever it was, it was so big that we both felt a gust of air at our backs. It could've been the size of the whole forest, the whole state of Tennessee. It could've been a god.

Judith dropped the light. It rattled and rolled, and she tripped as she tried to retrieve it.

"I've got it!" I swiped down and grabbed it, and I grabbed her elbow to lift her up and help her move. "Come on, I've got you too."

For a few seconds, I aimed the flashlight behind us. I wanted to see. I needed to see.

I saw.

It had a shape now, and color and depth. It was black and viscous, and it oozed onto the pavement of the little backwoods road that didn't even have a line in the middle to say that it had two lanes. It coiled and swirled. It breathed.

I swear to God, it breathed.

It was low to the ground, pooling and creeping. It moved around my car. It swallowed my car in an instant, and then I couldn't see it at all. I couldn't see anything on the other side of it either. It felt like the night itself was coming for us. We were caught in the undertow of something terrible and it was crawling toward us.

I stumbled, then untangled my knees and found the rhythm again, and kept going.

Could we outrun it? In the short term, probably. Could Judith keep moving long enough to ditch it? She was doing just fine. Hell, she was in the lead. I had to assume she was capable. I had to pray that I was too, but the burning in my lungs and the stitch in my side told me not to count on it.

I caught up to her and brought the light around our front again. I almost wished I hadn't.

With the help of my erratic flashlight, I saw the black ooze boiling at the edges of the woods on either side of us, coming forward toward the road's edge. Here and there, it dropped off and away, and I didn't know why. At the most distant, farthest edge of my hearing, I thought I detected a faint gurgling noise. I couldn't tell where it was coming from. I didn't know what it meant. It might not mean anything, but it stuck in my head regardless.

"What is it?" Judith asked the universe at large. She knew that I sure as shit didn't know. "What the hell is it?"

"Less talking! More fleeing!" I wheezed.

She nodded and I nodded back.

We jogged along where the center line ought to be. I waved the flashlight and tried not to look at the woods, around us, or behind us. There was nothing except for the town. No goal, no hope. The town would be a safe place to be. It had to be safe. It'd been safe all this time for everyone except Ellen. Hadn't it?

Just underneath that rushing cool air, a voice answered: Not exactly.

If I hadn't been so winded, I would've screamed. Instead, I tripped and fell; I caught myself on my hands and forced myself upright again. Judith had paused, doubled over. Her hands were on top of her knees, and she was panting. This was too much for her, and I knew it. But we had another half-mile to go, and the terrible black fog was still bubbling out of the trees. When the edge of the flashlight caught her face, my stomach clenched. She was flushed and sweating, and her eyes were bulging. This was too much for her. Hell, it was too much for me, and I lacked so much as the breath to say so.

But we weren't alone anymore. The night wasn't even dark anymore.

Meredith Barlow stood in the middle of the road.

She wore not the gray flowing shift I'd seen before, but the gleaming silver armor of a knight—helmet pushed up and back, perched on her head to show those vivid eyes. Her hair spilled out from underneath it, waving in a breeze I couldn't feel. She was so small, but her halo was so huge.

She glowed with the light of a burning witch. It was the light of a saint.

Some child of Joan's. The pope or the French girl; she could've claimed to serve either one and I would've believed her. Her lean white legs were bound in shining greaves, her tiny feet capped in sleek sabatons. In her hands, she held a sword that was nearly as long as she was tall.

She was luminous and terrible, beautiful and monstrous, Our Lady of the Terrible Night.

I dropped the flashlight.

She raised her sword.

She smashed it down onto the road, and the shockwave knocked me onto my ass. When I looked to my right, Judith was flat on her back, her eyes aimed at the stars and her mouth open. For one godawful second, I thought she was dead—absolutely beyond my reach forever—and I couldn't stand the thought of it. But then I saw she was breathing shallowly, and she blinked with a flutter of confusion.

I put out my hand toward her and she reached back, taking it. I crawled to her.

She sat up, and we clutched each other like children who were sharing the same nightmare.

The creeping force—or energy, or wave, or whatever it was—it stopped short, blown back by the same pulse that had thrown us to the ground. My flashlight was lying a few feet away, pointed back at the car. Not that I could actually see the car from where I was sitting; we'd run just far enough that even in broad daylight, it would've been beyond our vantage point. But I did see a watery, bleak mist lurking around us. It'd fenced us in. It surrounded us all, even our glorious, ghostly champion who stood with us against the night.

I clutched Judith as if I could save her, or she could save me. Somebody had to save somebody, or else what was the point? Why scribble the same message again and again, sending out that beacon to someone, somewhere, that a woman named Ellen was dead and gone, and none had come to claim her?

I refused to believe that it'd been a trap. I simply could not entertain the possibility that I'd been lured there with no hope of return.

Meredith Barlow wouldn't do that. Would she? She might have been a madwoman—or then again, probably not—but was she cruel?

I asked the shining phantasm, hoping and praying she was the hero I was counting on: "Can you hold it off alone?"

No, but that's all right. She shook her head, but she did it with a smile.

I didn't smile back. I was horrified. Judith crawled up tighter into my arms. She felt cold against me, and very frail. She was all bones and dust inside her clothes, and I tried not to hold her so tight that I'd break her. "What does that mean?" I begged the ghost. "Tell me what that means!"

Then she did the only thing that could've possibly reassured me that we weren't all about to die here, some of us for the first time: she winked at me.

Three women emerged from the darkness. They aligned beside her: Jillienne, Camille, and Liana. I might've been crazed with fear, but I swear their eyes were shining, reflecting the spirit's glow, or burning up from within, or something else. All I can say for certain is that I saw it and I believed it, and I knew for certain that we weren't caught in a trap after all.

With gentle apology written all over her face, Liana said, "I did try to warn you."

Camille added, "But sometimes if we warn too hard, we make it sound too interesting. That's the trick, you know? God, we really need to make ourselves more boring next time anyone shows up to ask."

Jillienne raised her hands. "If nothing else, we've got to stop being so goddamn hospitable."

"I could buy less tea?" Liana offered.

But the eldest of them demurred. "That is not an option." The rings on her fingers glittered in the spectral light. Then she commanded, "Closer!" in a loud, booming voice, and I hoped she wasn't addressing the dismal fog that crept up from all sides. "Here, at the road!"

But this time, she wasn't talking to the crawling murk or to her sisters, or to us either.

She was talking to all the other people.

They came out from behind the trio and the ghost; a dozen

women … two dozen women—more than that, I don't know—each one with a shovel slung over her shoulder. Some wore overalls, some wore jeans. Some wore dresses, but even those women wore mud boots. Several wore ponchos. I'd seen a few of them around the town.

Our waitress. Anne from the Rockford. Anne's sister. I'd never caught her name, or if I had, I'd forgotten it. Hell, in that moment I would've been hard-pressed to come up with my mother's name. The world was a midnight bonfire, and I was confused, exhausted, and aching, and still clinging to Judith.

One by one, the women filed off the road and disappeared between the trees.

I wanted to shout at them, to tell them it wasn't safe. I wanted to round them all up and herd them back to town where the thing might not follow us—or then again, it might. But that was stupid. They knew the danger better than I did, obviously. None of them looked frightened. In each, I saw resolve, confidence, and resignation. On a few, I saw annoyance, an expression like, "Here we go again, goddammit." At least one of them rolled her eyes at me. I couldn't blame her.

Within seconds, they were all gone.

A few seconds more, and a choir of shovels rang out, chiming off-beat in a minor key.

It was the jangling of beer can wind chimes, or the sharp clang of a blade hitting granite. The hard thump of stubborn roots that won't be easily cut. The shove and leverage of a foot pressing down, forcing a blade deeper.

Meredith Barlow rose off the road, her feet dangling even higher above the pavement. She held herself up like a lantern and her blinding, religious light was bright enough to serve every digger for a mile, even though the night was deep and haunted by far worse things than ghosts.

The shovels rose and the shovels fell, and feet pushed blades, and arms flung scoops of earth, and the holes deepened.

Camille and Liana ran to Judith and me. I waved them away, swore I was fine, staggered to my feet and dragged Judith with me. She was wobbly. They picked her up and she dangled between them, suspended by her armpits. Her feet found themselves and she walked, but slowly and weakly.

"It's only a few yards this way," I heard Liana say.

I asked, "What's only a few yards?"

Camille answered. "The town limits—the official border, and borders mean things. Even to forces like ..." she looked over her shoulder. "... that. It won't follow you past the boundary. It won't be strong enough to chase you now."

Liana nodded. "Between the three of us, we've warded the living daylights out of the town. It'll stay out here, don't worry. It's only a little farther. Come on, we can help."

"You always help, don't you?" I said, hardly any louder than a whisper.

She sighed. "It might be kinder to be wicked and run everybody off. But it's just not our nature." Camille agreed. "It never has been. Maybe when we're old and gray and batty. I think Jillienne is already seeding stories among the locals." Judith stumbled. The younger woman caught her. "I promise, we're almost there."

We passed the ghost and Jillienne Venterman, who scarcely gave us a glance. Her hands were still aloft, her jewelry dazzling in the supernatural light. Loud and clear, in a low, steady voice, she declared, "We are the ones who stand between the worlds. By no might and by no law—but by our will, and this alone—we choose to keep watch at these gates."

I checked over my shoulder again. I couldn't not look.

The blackness had thinned. It was draining away, siphoned off to either side of the road by the small but growing holes, dug by thirty or more silent women, a few yards away from the town limits of Cinderwich, Tennessee.

CHAPTER FOURTEEN

THE LADIES USHERED us back to the edge of Cinderwich where an old pickup truck was waiting—its engine running in a low, diesel rumble, and the dome light brightly lit inside the cab. Sitting behind the wheel was a grumpy-looking guy about my age with a buzzcut and a lot of vivid tattoos. Perched beside him behind the gearshift was a brown and white baby goat in a diaper. When the tattooed guy saw us, he leaned over to pop the passenger side door. He pulled the baby goat into his lap and said, "Get in already."

I decided to spare Judith the baby goat, so I climbed in first. I kind of wanted to pet it—circumstances be damned. If anything on earth could calm me down and make me feel better after the night we'd had, surely it was the soft snout of a baby goat. "Thanks," I said to the driver.

Judith mumbled "thanks" too, as Camille and Liana helped her inside.

When we were all inside and settled, Camille said, "Good night, Terror! Be a good baby!" Then she shut the door and smacked the hood. "Thank you, Shepherd."

"No worries. I've got 'em." He put the truck in gear, waited for the women to get out of the way, and drove us back toward the town square.

I held out a finger and scratched the goat's fuzzy little head. It was adorable, big-eyed and floppy-eared. "What's its name?" I asked.

"Terror."

"Terror?"

"That's what I said."

Shepherd wasn't very talkative, and Judith was leaning against the passenger window, wheezing quietly and staring into the night. I went ahead and shut up and let Terror suck happily on my fingers until we pulled into the Rockford parking lot.

Judith struggled to get out and I almost asked Shepherd if he'd go help her, since I was stuck in the middle, but she successfully escaped before it came to that. I shimmied sideways, untangling my legs from the shift and scooting gracelessly to the door.

"Thanks again," I said.

"You're welcome, but don't you pull that shit again."

"I'm sorry?"

Judith leaned against the truck. I sat with one ass cheek on the seat and one hanging free.

Shepherd said, "Next time somebody tells you to mind your business or leave, you take them at their word. I don't care how good the tea is."

"I will do exactly that," I vowed.

"Don't worry about your car. It'll start up fine in the morning, I bet. And nobody will bother it between now and then—I can promise you that."

"But I called a tow truck …"

"Somebody will un-call it. Get inside, stay in your room, and try to get some rest. Everything will be fine—at least until the dark of night rolls around again. By then, you two had better be someplace else."

Just loudly enough to be heard inside the truck, Judith replied, "That won't be a problem."

"Good. Head on out and let us take care of our own. We know what we're doing."

I dropped to the ground and shut the door behind myself. I waved to Shepherd and Terror and put an arm around Judith.

Together, we went inside.

The lobby was as empty and quiet as a tomb. Victoria Barlow

glared her customary glare. A small TV on the hotel's concierge desk was tuned to a local network station with the volume turned all the way down. It was airing a rerun of a cop show I hadn't watched in a while. Except for one lamp, the screen was the only other light.

In one of the cubbies behind the desk, several envelopes were rolled up, awaiting their delivery. I stepped behind the desk and checked, since there was nobody to ask for help. Everyone was out in the woods, digging holes, draining the evil away, letting it settle back into the earth. Is that what they were doing? It made as much sense as anything else.

None of the messages were for us.

The hall to our room was grim, illuminated only by the exit sign at the end. The fixture on the ceiling had either burned out or been turned off. Maybe Cinderwich had some kind of early warning system that alerted everybody to a threat outside the town limits. No sirens, but dimmed lights and emergency signs, like mood music in a video game.

Sure, why not.

Inside our room, both beds had been made while we were out. (I don't know who did it. I hadn't seen any housekeeping workers at any point on any day of our stay.) Everything else was just as we'd left it. My side of the sink with my toiletries. Judith's side of the sink with hers. My open suitcase on the floor beside my bed. Judith's closed neatly, upright beside hers.

She sat at the foot of her bed and flopped back.

"Judy, are you okay?"

"I'll live. Still catching my breath though."

"Okay." I sat on the foot of my bed too and picked up the TV remote. I found something benign—a PBS special on Antarctica, I think. There was a lot of snow and chatter about glaciers, that's all I remember. I left the volume down at a loud whisper and laid back flat on the bed, just like Judith.

"Hey, Kate."

"Yeah?" I asked, rolling my head to look at her.

"Where's that bottle of Bulleit?"

I sat up again. It hurt more than I expected. It was on the night-stand between our beds. "I'll get it. I'll, um ... I'll find us some cups too." We'd thrown away the plastic ones, but I didn't see that they'd been replaced.

"I don't need a cup."

"Seriously?"

"Give me the goddamn bottle and don't ask silly questions."

"Yes ma'am," I said, and handed it over without further protest.

Between us, we killed it off in less than an hour. After that, we fell asleep. I don't know how. Sufficient alcohol and exhaustion, or else we were just shutting down in the wake of something unfathomable. Were we in shock? I've never seen anything more shocking in my life, and I strongly doubt that Judith had. Were we just knackered? Equally likely. We'd both done more running in that one hour than either of us had done in years. Never mind all the screaming.

Either way, when the sun came up, we were still wearing our clothes from the night before.

I hadn't shut the curtains all the way, so morning came streaming in, smacking me in the face. My head ached. I smelled like hell. My palms were scraped up, and I'm not sure when that happened exactly. Could've been at any point. Hell, it was a wonder that I had any skin on my hands or knees left at all, considering.

Judith was halfway wrapped up in the throw blanket that had been folded neatly on the bottom of her bed. She'd forgotten her eye mask, but she was facing away from the window and the light hadn't pestered her awake yet.

I heard a very, very quiet noise by the door. I sat up and saw yet another piece of paper, freshly slipped underneath it.

Grudgingly, I hauled myself upright. Everything cracked. Everything hurt. My mouth stank. I could taste it. I picked up the folded note, half expecting to see familiar handwriting. It could be another vague clue or another baffling bit of nonsense.

But no. It was only our bill with the word "Thanks!" scrawled across the hotel's letterhead. They already had my credit card information, and Anne must've run it through the system. A receipt was stapled to the back. All we had to do was load Judith's car, drive back to mine, and get the hell out of town.

I had no good reason to believe Shepherd, that my car would start up without any trouble. I had no good reason to disbelieve him either; and if he was wrong? If the tow truck had hauled it off already ... well ... I'd have to spend part of the day on the phone with AAA. Or something. I chose to believe that it was still sitting there beside the road. I chose to believe that it would start with an ordinary twist of the key, and I planned my exit accordingly.

I went to the bathroom, peeling off my clothes as I walked and tossing them around the room. Onto my bed. Onto the floor. On top of the TV, which we'd never turned off. I didn't mess with it. If Judith wanted it off, she could turn it off herself.

The shower came on with a squeak and a spit. I adjusted the temperature and stood there barefoot and naked in front of the mirror, waiting for steam to fill the room. But there was nothing new on the mirror. No clues, no parting wishes. Nothing but the swiped streaks I'd left with the hand towel when I'd erased Meredith's missive.

I felt like something was over, or at least our part in it was finished. No one had anything left to whisper to us or fresh information to taunt us with. Cinderwich was done with us, that's how it felt.

Into the shower I went.

The water was almost hot enough to scald, but I liked it that way and I cranked it up. I unwrapped a thumb-sized sample of soap and stood there in the water, smelling vanilla and mint, I think. The spray and the steam felt good. Everything still ached, but I had hot water and soap. Everything would be fine now. The adventure had concluded. Except.

What had Meredith meant?

I put Ellen in the blackgum tree.

Yeah, but why? Had she been trying to save her? Protect her from the crawling sludge? If we'd been able to climb a tree the night before, we might've escaped it. Or not. Is that what Ellen tried to do, climb out of its reach?

Ellen might have been drunk or sick. She might've been caught by the sludge, and Meredith had been too late to help. She might've been dead when Meredith found her. Maybe the little ghost had only wanted to lift her up so that somebody might find her. Maybe she'd fished her out of a hole. Not everyone can see a clootie well, but if anyone can, surely, it's the dead.

Did anybody in Cinderwich know?

When we'd spoken to the Ventermans and Liana, I hadn't felt like they were lying. Leaving out parts of the truth, clearly. But they'd been small children when Ellen died. They had never been part of the crime (if that's what it was), only the aftermath and the coverup. "So much gray area," I said under my breath.

They knew how to handle whatever came from the water, and that was the important bit.

Well, it was one of the important bits. It was the one that'd saved our lives—I was sure of it. If that disgusting black mass had caught us—if it'd wrapped around our feet and pulled us to the ground, if it'd poured itself down our throats—Meredith might've had to stick us up in the trees too.

But it hadn't come to that.

We were alive. We were in shitty shape, and when I turned off the water, I could hear Judith snoring through the door.

I took my time in the bathroom. I even did my makeup, standing there in a towel after I'd wiped the mirror dry. Every time I leaned close for detail work with my eyeliner pen or mascara, I half-expected to see the dark-haired sprite grinning back at me, her finger held to her lips.

But the mirror was only a mirror.

Finally, Judith woke up and was stirring around. I lounged on the bed with the remote while she pulled herself together, suggesting breakfast or lunch at the McDonald's near the Waffle House. She grunted in agreement, but otherwise didn't talk much.

Neither one of us wanted to eat in town. Or be in town. We wanted out and away.

When we were all packed up, we each took our respective purses and suitcases and rolled for the door. I found the empty bottle of rye on the floor. I kicked it under the bed because fuck it, that's why.

No one was at the front desk. We dragged our luggage past it without even looking twice to see if Anne was there to say goodbye.

Judith used the key fob to unlock her rental. We piled in. We dug our sunglasses out of our bags and put them on. They wouldn't totally hide the hangovers and exhaustion, but they were a satisfactory disguise for the moment.

I fastened my seatbelt. "Okay. Let's go get my car. Let's get the hell out of here."

"Yeah." She pulled down the visor and a pack of cigarettes dropped out. She tapped one free and popped it into her mouth, then pushed the car's lighter until it clicked. When it was sufficiently red-hot, she lit the cigarette and rolled her window down. "Let's do that."

But before we reached the turn-off for the road where I'd left my stalled car, I saw the library ahead on our right. "Hey, wait."

"No."

"Seriously Judith, wait. Can't we stop, just for a minute? I never made it to the periodicals."

She sighed, the cigarette dangling Bogart-style from her bottom lip. "So?"

"So, it's the one thing we said we were going to do that we didn't do. I'm an academic completist. Humor me. The sun's up and everything. We'll be fine. I promise we'll be fine. The ladies even said so, right? Broad daylight and all that shit. Nothing can hurt us now."

"Jesus, you're assuming a lot ..." she grumbled, but she turned into the parking lot of the little branch library anyway. "And what do you want with the periodicals?"

"At first, I wanted to check out contemporary newspaper records, see if there were any details to Ellen's case that had kind of been forgotten over the years. And besides, you wanted to look up fresh info about the freemasons, or that's what I thought."

"I don't care about the masons anymore, Kate. I just want to leave."

"So do I," I assured her. "But I've got another idea, and if I don't chase it, I'll never forgive myself."

She sighed and unbuckled her seatbelt. "Do tell."

We climbed out into the cool morning air and blinked because the light was just too damn much. Judith rubbed her barely smoked cigarette against a concrete planter to kill the coal and save the rest, then left it in the car.

I led the way to the front door, opened it, and held it for her. "Something's been bugging me. That picture your assistant sent— the one with the masonic ceremony or whatever."

"I said I don't care anymore," she protested weakly. Then before I could press the issue, she gave up and asked, "What about it?"

"Besides the fact it's kind of fucked up?" Someone whispered shhh, so I lowered my voice. "Melody said she couldn't find any additional information on the subject, but maybe we can find some here, in Analog Land. Not everything has been digitized everywhere. You know that as well as I do. I'll go find a sign-in log and see if they'll let me poke around in their old strips."

She nodded, suddenly thoughtful instead of grizzled. "All right. Actually, that gives me an idea."

"A good idea? Bad idea?"

"Just an idea. Go ahead." She waved toward the sign that said Periodicals.

"Aren't you coming with me?"

"I told you," she said. "I have an idea. You do your thing; I'll go do mine."

"Don't leave me here, Judy. I'd never forgive you. I swear to God, if I leave the periodicals room and your rental is missing from that lot—"

"I'm not leaving," she vowed as she walked away.

"You promise!" I whispered as loud as I dared. Then, more to myself than anybody else, I said like a mantra, "She promises. She'll still be here. I'll circle back around in a few minutes. She won't go anywhere. She won't leave me."

I opened the door to the periodicals room where everything was cold and smelled like plastic. I saw a sign-in log, so I put my name down with the date and time and took a look around. Several machines for reading microfilm and microfiche were lined against a wall, relics from the Cold War, each and every one.

The boxes of relevant media were all stashed in cabinets that were taller than me, but the drawers I wanted were within reach, and before long, I'd found the archives for the local paper, circa 1956. Nothing in the room went back to 1856, except for old property and church records, but I went out on a limb and picked the 100-year anniversary of the event. The trains would've still been running back then. Maybe there was another ceremony. Maybe the remaining Barlows were part of it.

The Cinderwich Sentinel had too many syllables for my liking, and it wasn't organized terribly well, but it was short because not much had ever happened in Cinderwich.

After half an hour of sifting through plastic wheels of film pulled from dusty boxes and sticking drawers, I had to admit that I'd hit a dead end. Somewhere in my gut, I had a very strong feeling that the ceremony had something to do with whatever had followed and whatever remained.

But even if I was right, I couldn't prove it. The archives were not merely too primitive, they were too sparse. I was out of luck.

I stood up and put away the last spools like a good library citizen and only then wondered where the hell Judith had gone off to. It'd been more than a minute since we'd parted company.

I left the periodicals room and shut the door, scanning the library for some sign of her.

The building was as silent as a tomb. No rustling pages, no squeaking wheels of library carts, no dull footsteps from the orthopedic shoes of quiet librarians. No air conditioner humming. No patrons asking for the restroom.

No Judith.

She wasn't in any of the common areas, the little landing with the comfy chairs, or in the restroom when I checked it. Then I went aisle by aisle, not wanting to holler for her even though I think we were the only people in there. I mean, someone had hissed at me to shush when we first came in, but it must have been a librarian.

Wait, there Judith was. I'd found her.

I saw her through a window in what must have been a conference room or some such. I leaned around the door, knocking softly. "Hey, lady. No luck for me. Are you ready to pack it in?"

She was seated at a desk surrounded by 3-ring binders that were covered in dust. I could tell by the fingerprints which ones she'd opened already and which ones she hadn't gotten to just yet.

"Judith?"

"You gave me an idea," she said again. "What you said about the sign-in sheet. I was thinking, if Ellen ever did come here, if she was the woman found in the tree, surely, she would've stopped at the library. She didn't have a library card, or at least … not one she could use here. But she could've talked her way into the local history archives. Her student ID would've helped. She still carried it with her like an AWOL soldier who hasn't tossed his uniform just in case he changes his mind. Just a student doing research for a project, that's all."

"I don't get it. What does a library card have to do with anything?"

She waved at binders spread over the table. "Library card or none, she still would've had to sign for any box she opened."

I was tired, that's all I can say. That's why it took me a few seconds longer than it should have, to realize what she was saying. "Holy shit, Judith. You found something."

She smiled down at the paperwork. "I can hardly believe they still have these records, but you know how archivists are. You know what they do. If there's room for it, they'll keep it. Even if ..."

I pulled up a chair and sat down beside her. "Even if they have to make room?"

"Every single time, yes. Nothing so trivial that it should be tossed, and no scrap so pointless that it shouldn't be saved. It's in their bones, I think. Ellen's bones too. Probably yours as well."

"So you thought why not check."

Her eyes were wet, and her hands were shaking. "How many people could have possibly signed for media in this one stupid month that she vanished, all the way back in 1977?" Her voice froze, her fingers dangling over the page before her. "I mean, she wouldn't have stayed here for weeks without telling me. She wouldn't have ... have moved to town without so much as a telegram or a phone call. She wasn't here long. She couldn't have been. She wouldn't have done that to me."

With a lump in my throat, I asked, "Judith, how many names are on the sign-in list?"

In reply, she turned the binder around so I could see what was written inside it: a short list of signatures, and on one line, a familiar line of letters in unfamiliar handwriting. It was a stranger's treatment of my own signature, if I ever used my first name, but I never did, and no one ever called me that. Sometimes I even forgot about it. But Judith never did.

She exhaled almost fifty years' worth of waiting, and she said, "Six, including yours."

ACKNOWLEDGMENTS

A book never makes it to the shelves without a whole host of helpful folks behind the scenes, and this one is no exception … though I'll keep this short. First, I must thank the three gorgeous, brilliant women who inspired my fictional "ladies." They know who they are, and if you know them, well. You might recognize them. Next, big thanks to all the usual suspects—my agent, Stacia Decker, Apex's own dear Mr. Sizemore (who published one of my very first short stories, a very long time ago), and my husband—who keeps the lights on while I try to write books. Thanks also to a secret little internet group where the stratospheric femmes throw one back, every now and again, and my eternal gratitude to Shepherd—who went rummaging through his brainmeats to help me with some of the historic background on this one. You're all marvelous, and I couldn't have done it without you.

© *Libby Bulloff*

CHERIE PRIEST is the author of two dozen books and novellas, most recently the Booking Agents mysteries *Grave Reservations* and *Flight Risk*. She also wrote gothic horror projects *The Toll*, *The Family Plot*, and the Philip K. Dick nominee *Maplecroft*; but she is perhaps best known for the steampunk pulp adventures of the Clockwork Century, beginning with *Boneshaker*. Cherie lives in Seattle, WA, with her husband and a menagerie of exceedingly photogenic pets.

DON'T WAIT! *SCAN THE CODE* **AND FEED YOUR IMAGINATION!**

FIND MORE GREAT BOOKS AT APEXBOOKCOMPANY.COM